DATE DUE

OC 25 48	FEB 6 85	NO 11 9	
NOV 08 79	FE 25 '86	JA 15 '0	
DEC 5 79	DE 19 '86	O 31 '04	
DEC 20 '79	JA 12 '87		
JAN 10 '80	AP 9 '87		
JAN 24 '80	DE 29 '8		
FEB 11 '80	JA 31 '90		
MR 21 '80	SE 10 '9		
APR 4 '80	JY 26 '9		
MAY 12 '80			
FE 28 '81	NO 6 '91		
JAN 14 '82	DE 17 '92		

Treasure in Hell's Canyon

Treasure in Hell's Canyon

BILL GULICK

DOUBLEDAY & COMPANY, INC.
GARDEN CITY, NEW YORK
1979

All of the characters in this book are fictitious,
and any resemblance to actual persons, living or dead,
is purely coincidental.

Library of Congress Cataloging in Publication Data

Gulick, Grover C
    Treasure in Hell's Canyon.

    I. Title.
PZ3.G94427Tr [PS3557.U43]   813'.5'2
ISBN: 0-385-09848-0
Library of Congress Catalog Card Number 78-20235

To the memory of H.W.W. "Bill" Johnson, a big man, with a big heart, who shared his love for the Snake River with so many of us—and whose irrepressible spirit still may be heard chuckling in every white-water rapid in Hell's Canyon.

—Bill Gulick

A thick blanket of fog covered Portland, stilling boat traffic on the Willamette River, shrouding gaslights to a sickly yellow glow on the streets leading up from the wharves. Though the hour was only half past five, the gray gloom of the late February afternoon already was giving way to the deep blackness of night.

Standing at the open casement windows of his upstairs law office with a half-finished drink in his hand, Walt Randall spoke over his shoulder to his brother Allan, who was sitting in a chair beside the desk.

"You're heading upriver tomorrow?"

"Yeah. If this fog lifts, we'll be on our way at dawn."

"Aboard the *Wide West?*"

"Right. I've booked passage for two. Just say the word, I'll make it for three."

A tall, slim, well-coordinated man in his late twenties, Walt Randall had a lean, craggy, not quite handsome face. His eyes were dark and at times moody; in them, the mental alertness of an experienced attorney, the cynicism of a man with no illusions about human nature, and the impulsiveness of a man with a reckless disregard for the cut-and-dried rules of life were strangely mixed. Turning away from the window, he finished his drink, crossed to the desk, and motioned at his brother's empty glass.

"A refill?"

"No, thanks. I'm meeting Lord Smythe at the Willamette Hotel for supper in a few minutes. He likes a few belts before he eats. And while he eats. And after he eats. If I'm going to match him drink for drink and keep my wits about me, I want to start even." He smiled wryly. "I don't absorb booze as well as I used to, Walt. Old age, I guess."

A twinge of regret for the lost innocence of the childhood they had shared touched Walt as he gazed at his brother, who was ten years his senior. Though his body still was thick and powerful, Allan had developed a noticeable paunch. Though his face still was handsome, his wavy black hair was turning gray. The usually friendly twinkle around his eyes was tempered with lines of worry now, and his once-natural exuberance at times seemed forced. Half a lifetime spent vainly chasing rainbows had taken its toll.

"You really think Lord Farley Windham Smythe is the genuine article?" Walt asked quietly.

"You bet! He represents the biggest mining syndicate in the world. South Africa, Peru, Mexico, India—if there's gold, silver, or copper in the country, his company has holdings there."

"The West is full of phoney Englishmen, Allan. How do you know he's for real?"

"I've checked on him with half a dozen reliable mining people. His credentials are impeccable. He's been in the United States scouting out hard-rock mining prospects for six months. On his recommendation alone, his syndicate will risk half a million dollars in development money."

"Will it take that much to get the Golden Girl in production?"

"It probably will. Hell's Canyon is a rugged, inaccessible place. But the Golden Girl is rich, Walt! Why, the sample I showed Lord Smythe assayed eight hundred dollars a ton."

"Hand-sorted or run of the vein?"

"Well, of course it was hand-sorted!" Allan exclaimed, getting up out of his chair and restlessly moving about the room. "Do you expect me to move a hundred tons of ore four hundred miles downriver so that he can look at it? Do I have to prove I've struck it rich before you'll move your ass out of this office, come upriver, and take a look at what I've found? Is working for that Chinese dope peddler making you so much money that you refuse to take a chance on a real piece of dough—?"

"Whoa, now!" Walt interrupted sharply. "I don't work for a dope peddler. I work for the Chen Yu Importing Company. And I didn't say I wasn't interested in your gold mine. All I said was I can't go upriver with you now."

"You called Lord Smythe a phoney."

"No, I didn't. All I said was that the possibility should be considered." Walt's voice softened. "For your sake, I hope you *have* hit it rich, Allan. I hope that his syndicate *will* spend half a million dollars developing your mine. Lord knows, for all the years you've spent in those gopher holes of yours, you deserve some reward."

"Can you have supper with us tonight?" Allan pleaded. "I'd like you to meet Lord Smythe."

"Sorry. I've got a prior engagement with Chen Yu."

"But you will come upriver before too long and take a look at the Golden Girl?"

"Why don't you drop me a line and let me know what your British friend thinks of your mine, after he's had a look? If his opinion is favorable and his company is willing to put some money into it, you'll need legal representation to draw up the papers. I'll be happy to come upriver and help out then."

"We'll have to organize a big company and sell a lot of stock," Allan said eagerly. "We'll have to elect a board of directors. If you'll handle the legal work, we'll cut you in for a piece of the action. Then you can tell Chen Yu to take his importing business and stuff it."

"For the past two years, Chen Yu has paid me at least a thousand dollars a month for handling his affairs," Walt said. "When you can do as well, I'll consider working with you. Meanwhile, we both have appointments to keep. Let me close up the office and turn out the lamps. I'll walk a couple of blocks with you."

Pulling the windows to and latching them, Walt lifted a gunbelt, holster, and a .38 caliber Smith and Wesson revolver off a coatrack standing in one corner of the room. As he fitted the belt around his waist, he heard the street door at the foot of the stairs open and close. Allan gave him a questioning look.

"Expecting somebody?"

"No."

Firm, heavy, slow steps of a man mounting the stairs became audible. Walt opened the door of the office and peered down into the gloom. Recognizing the visitor from the sounds he was making even before seeing him clearly, he called out a cheerful greeting.

"Hi, Mac! How are you?"

Puffing harshly as he reached the top landing, Inspector James McClure, United States Customs and Immigration Bureau, came into the office. Red-faced, flat-footed, and fifty, McClure carried twenty more pounds of weight than were good for him; he looked flabby and soft; but, as Walt had good reason to know, there was no fat between his ears.

"Butting into a family conference?" McClure inquired, nodding to Allan, whom he knew.

"No, we just finished," Allan said. He shook Walt's hand. "When we get back from Hell's Canyon, I'll drop you a line. If the news is good, I'll expect you to come upriver to Lewiston on the next boat. See you, Mac."

As Allan clumped down the stairs, Inspector McClure's gaze dropped to the gunbelt which Walt was adjusting around his waist.

"Looking for an ornery client?"

"This is my poker night and I usually win," Walt said with a smile. "When I'm out late and carrying a lot of gold, I always pack a gun. Lots of lazy Irishmen in town, these days, who would rather steal than work."

Inspector McClure, who was Irish, responded with a grimace, then, at Walt's hand gesture of invitation, lowered his bulk into the leather chair at one end of the attorney's desk.

"We've got to have a talk, Walt."

"Official or unofficial?"

"What the hell's the difference?" Inspector McClure grunted testily. "You know who I work for. I know who you work for. We never lie to each other. So fix me a drink and let's have a talk."

Getting a clean glass tumbler, Walt poured two generous drinks, sat down behind his desk, and gazed at the Customs and Immigration officer.

"Fire away, Mac."

"You do a lot of legal work for the Chen Yu Importing Company."

"Yes, I do."

"Chen Yu is the richest, most powerful Chinese merchant in Portland. He's head of the inner council that runs a benevolent society called the Sam Yup Company. During the past six months, he's sponsored and brought into the United States—by my count—fifty-six Chinamen—"

"Legally, Mac. I checked their papers."

"Yeah, I know. They all belonged to the merchant, student, or professional class. They all had exit certificates from South China and entry permits into the United States. Chen Yu swore that they all were nephews of his and would not do any kind of work that would compete with American labor. All crap, of course."

"But legal crap. What's your complaint?"

"I've got good reason to believe that some of those 'nephews' he's bringing in are 'nieces.' I've got good reason to believe they're going into the trade of prostitution. And that *is* illegal."

"We both know the facts of life, Mac," Walt said in as diplomatic a way as he could manage. "Where men go, women will follow. You can no more stop prostitution among the Chinese in America than you can stop it among the Irish, Dutch, and Swedes. Furthermore, 'good reason to believe' is not proof. Do you have any proof?"

"That he's importing girls?" McClure snorted. "How could I have? The way male and female Chinese dress alike when they're traveling, there ain't no way I can get proof—unless I make 'em strip."

Walt smiled. "Aren't you empowered to do that?"

"Sure, I am—just like a Chinese official in Canton is empowered to order a lady missionary to take off her clothes because he suspects her of being a man. But people don't take kindly to stripping before strangers. If I pulled a stunt like that, Chen Yu would complain to the State Department, and the same thing would happen to me that would happen to a Chinese official dumb enough to make a lady missionary strip—I'd lose my head."

"What do you want me to do—ask Chen Yu to close all the red-light houses in the Chinese quarter?"

"That would help some. But the main thing he's got to do right now is squelch the rumor that's floating around town. Because if that auction comes off as advertised, the Immigration Bureau and the Portland Police Department won't have no choice but to make a raid. In these times, you know what that could lead to."

"Auction?" Walt Randall said with a frown. "What kind of an auction?"

"Girls. Fifteen-year-old virgins. Six of 'em, just brought in from China, guaranteed to be the best merchandise available, money back if not satisfied. Talk is, they'll be put on the block at two o'clock Sunday afternoon. Guessing is, they'll bring two or three thousand dollars apiece. Every rich Chinaman in Portland plans to be there." Shaking his head as Walt started to refill his tumbler, Inspector McClure heaved his bulk out of his chair. "If that auction comes off, Walt, the bluenoses and radicals are bound to hear about it. Then we'll have to raid. And the fat will be in the fire."

"Thanks for the warning, Mac," Walt said as he rose and showed the inspector to the door. "I'll see Chen within the hour."

2

By long-established custom, the Chen Yu Importing Company settled Walt Randall's bill for services rendered on the final Friday of each month. Payment always was made in raw gold, precisely weighed on a set of brass scales in Chen Yu's office. Other than Walt Randall's verbal statement of the amount due and Chen Yu's payment of that sum, no bill was submitted, no receipt requested, no record made. For what both men felt were valid reasons, their relationship was kept unostentatious and discreet.

In his quiet, well-mannered way, Chen Yu had made it clear from the beginning that he expected the attorney who looked after his company's interests in the Pacific Northwest to visit him promptly at six o'clock on that particular Friday evening each month, collect the fee he had earned, then linger until midnight or so for a few hours of polite conversation, mellow drink, a delectable supper, and a friendly poker game in which Chen would try in oriental earnest to win back the gold. This Walt did not mind, for the Chinese merchant played with more zest than skill. Like most oriental gamblers Walt had known, Chen played hunches rather than odds, trusted in luck rather than logic, and would rather bet on a second-best hand and lose money than fold it and lose face—thus was an adversary to be cherished.

Tonight, he would be taking $1,250 into the game, Walt mused as he walked along fog-shrouded Front Street toward the Chinese quarter, for the services he had rendered the Chen Yu Importing Company during the past month had been substantial. By mutual agreement, Chen would bring an equal amount of gold to the table; the chips with which they would play would be valued at one, five, and ten dollars; and the game would end either at midnight or when one of them lost all the gold he had brought into the room.

Exasperation mixed with alarm tightened the lines of Walt's face. Shrewd merchant and transparent poker player though he was, Chen Yu could be very dense and murky when it came to comprehending his attorney's repeated warnings that there were some import restrictions that could not be circumvented, some officials who could not be persuaded to overlook violations of the Alien Registration laws, and some oriental attitudes toward women that, while normal and accepted in China, would be certain to stir up a hornet's nest of public indignation if called to the attention of Portland's religious leaders, women's rights crusaders, or, worst of all, Workingmen's Party rabble-rousers searching for a cause to mount and ride into City Hall or the Oregon Legislature.

Sure, any sensible man would admit that it had been grossly unfair to force a treaty on China whose terms guaranteed protection of the lives and property of Americans doing business, saving souls, or traveling as tourists in the Orient, while in the United States drunken mobs of Irishmen, Swedes, Italians, Welshmen, Germans, and heterogeneous mixtures thereof proclaiming themselves "Workingmen" rioted and murdered in Rock Springs, pillaged and burned in Seattle, Tacoma, and other parts of the West, and hysterically screamed aloud and in print: *"The Chinese must go!"*

Any sensible man also would admit that as cooks, laundrymen, woodchoppers, tailors, gardeners, miners, or in any other occupation that demanded persistence, patience, stamina, and skill, the Chinese could not be equaled as workers. There probably was not a middle- or upper-class household in Portland that did not employ a Chinese cook, houseboy, or gardener.

True, among themselves the Chinese did engage in brawls and commit violent crimes. But Walt could not recall a single instance of a Chinaman attacking a white man or woman or

getting involved in a crime against the whites more serious
than petty theft. Yes, any sensible man who was not out of
work or under the influence of the Workingmen's Party radicals would admit that Portland's Chinese behaved themselves
pretty well, provided a dependable source of cheap labor, and
were an asset to the community.

But let the word be spread that a slave market existed in
the heart of Portland's Chinatown, where fifteen-year-old girls
were being sold into a life of sin—stripped naked, mind you,
stark, jaybird naked, then paraded back and forth on a raised
platform so that they could be carefully examined for defects
by potential buyers—let *that* story be broadcast and magnified
by the radicals—a sensible man would be hard to find.

"If they will auction off their own daughters," the rabble-
rousers would demand of outraged crowds, "what will the
yellow devils do to *your* daughters, if they get them in their
clutches? This couldn't happen, you say? Oh, my friends, how
little you know of the devious ways of the oriental mind! A
sleeping potion slipped into a glass of milk; a cloth saturated
with chloroform; a child lured away from a family picnic in
the woods . . ."

Utter nonsense, of course, Walt brooded as he turned right
into Second Street, which led up from the river into the Chinese quarter. Peering into the gloom of the poorly lit street, he
adjusted the holster to a more comfortable position on his right
hip under his coat. From his own experience, the most dangerous districts in Portland were those frequented by "Workingmen." When a man of that class got a few drinks under his
belt and turned mean, he respected neither law nor race; he
would commit mayhem against anybody.

The point he must get across to Chen Yu tonight, Walt
brooded, was that there were limits to the Chinese customs
that could be imported with impunity. Openly selling young
virgins to the highest bidder was too flagrant a violation of
American morality to be ignored by the authorities; they
would be compelled to take drastic action. Not that a Chinatown raid by immigration officers and the Portland police

would have a chance of producing evidence that would stand up in court. Thanks to an intricate system of guards, multiple doors, floor exits, and labyrinthian passageways, any number of Chinamen packed into a room for a female slave auction would disperse and vanish, along with the girls, long before the minions of the law could chop their way through the doors.

No, the damage would be done later—after word of the raid and the reason for it had spread—by mobs of self-righteous white citizens carrying torches, clubs, axes, guns, and explosives. Economic depression gripped the country. Times were slow and work was scarce. Many of the day laborers being laid off were Irish, men with loud mouths, quick tempers, a thirst for strong drink, and a tendency to act before they thought. During recent weeks, a number of petty acts of violence had been committed against the Chinese. Given a moral indignity that demagogues of *all* creeds, classes, and races could denounce, the unorganized mob quickly would turn into a monster.

Vaguely outlined in the gloom at the far corner of the block, a story-and-a-half board-and-batten Chinese washhouse stood perched against a hillside. Orange lamplight shone through the windows of its upper floor; dark shadows lay under its lower story, which was raised on stilts three feet above the level of the ground.

As he drew nearer, Walt saw a small point of flame suddenly blossom in the shadows at street level. Someone had struck a match. In the flame's brief glow, he got a glimpse of the profile of a kneeling man. Walt's skin prickled. The man appeared to be holding a bundle, from which a foot or so of string depended. String? No, a fuse, for a shower of sparks sputtered from it now as the bundle was tossed under the building. The figure straightened, turned, and started running up the street.

"You!" Walt yelled. "Hold up!"

The man stopped, turned back, crouched. An orange streak of fire lanced toward Walt. A pistol barked. A gob of mud torn out of the street plastered his face, half blinding him, and he could hear a bullet buzzing off into the distance.

Wiping the mud out of his eyes with his left hand, he pushed back his coattails with his right hand and drew the Smith and Wesson. Kneeling, he aimed carefully, then fired twice. At the second shot, the man, who had gotten to his feet and started running, stumbled, recovered his balance, and kept going.

Then the street erupted in an earth-shaking blast of noise and an eye-searing flare of light. . . .

3

Whether the force of the explosion or his own belated reflex action sprawled him full length in the street, Walt Randall did not know. All he knew was that he was lying facedown in wet, cold, gooey mud. A shower of debris was falling around him; in imagination, he could picture boards, nails, flatirons, bodies, and shards of glass flying through the air. Since the nape of his neck was his most vulnerable spot, he covered it with his left hand, while under his chest his right hand kept a tight grip on the revolver.

Most of the debris that rained down on him was light, but twice he was struck by falling objects whose impact made him grunt with pain. One hit him on the left shoulder blade, the other on the right hip. Then at last the artificial rain stopped. Groggily, he rolled over and sat up. With his ears still ringing from the noise of the blast, he assessed the damages done to his physical person. Other than the contusions on his left shoulder and right hip, whose seriousness he could judge only by feel, he seemed to be unhurt.

Shakily, he got to his feet. Staring at what had been a Chinese washhouse a few moments ago, he saw a disorderly tangle of splintered boards, fit only for a bonfire. Despite the dampness of the night, fire now was crackling at several places in the pile, which could only mean that the kerosene lamps used to illumine the upper-story workroom, and perhaps extra cans of inflammable fluid stored beneath the building, had been ignited by the blast. That any person in the washhouse could have survived the explosion seemed incredible; yet survive they had, for a dozen or so black-clad, pigtailed figures were scurrying around the wreckage, screaming and gesticulating, as unintelligible, frantic, and purposeless as a flock of chickens whose roost has been struck by lightning.

Three limp figures being dragged away from the burning wreckage by their clansmen appeared to be badly hurt. From buildings on either side, swarms of Chinese had appeared, carrying shovels, buckets of water, and wet sacks, with which they were attacking the flames. Somewhere in the gabble of excited Cantonese, a shrill voice shouted in pidgin English.

"Gettee fly en-jun! Hurry up, chop-chop, gettee fly en-jun!"

Fire House Number One, boasted to be Portland's finest, was located on Front Street, just two blocks away. Though seldom called upon to extinguish house fires in weather as damp as this, the two-man crew, the steam pressure pumper, the team of horses, and the ingenious harness that could be dropped upon them and the fire engine in a matter of seconds, would be ready and eager to answer the call, backed by a brigade of enthusiastic volunteers.

Pigtail flying, a skinny, sallow-faced young Chinaman burst out of the crowd and came toward Walt at a dead run. Seeing him standing in the middle of the street, the Chinese youth gave a shriek of fright, leaped sideways, and fell. His face contorted with fear, the young Oriental skittered crablike around and past Walt, his terror-stricken eyes never leaving the gun in Walt's hand, until he reached the boardwalk on the far side of the street, then he wheeled and vanished into the darkness. Only then did Walt realize what a menacing figure he must appear to be.

"Hell!" he muttered to himself. "He thinks I did it!"

Without bothering to wipe the mud off the Smith and Wesson, he holstered it. Leaving the mud on his face as the best possible disguise, he turned into a side street, putting the light, activity, and confusion of the burning washhouse behind him. What he had witnessed was yet another senseless act of violence against a defenseless people. In all likelihood, several Chinese had been seriously hurt or killed by the dynamite bomb. Certainly they had been frightened out of their wits, which had been the bomber's intent.

Too bad I didn't kill the cowardly bastard, Walt mused grimly. But it would not help the Chinese or bring Walt himself anything but trouble if he stayed until the police arrived on the scene. What could he tell them? That he had seen a man light and throw the bomb; that he had yelled at him, been shot at, and had returned two shots himself, one of which, he suspected, had struck the bomber's leg. All that would accomplish would be to publicize his own name in newspaper accounts of the outrage, while the identity of the bomber remained a mystery. Better to vanish and keep his mouth shut.

Behind him, down on Front Street, the big brass bell on the roof of Fire House Number One began clanging stridently in the fog-shrouded dark. . . .

Never since Walt Randall had known him had Chen Yu expressed personal anger against the way his countrymen in America were being treated by the white radicals. A plump, round-faced, pale-skinned man in his mid-forties, Chen smiled a great deal and always seemed to have his feelings under perfect control. But tonight, listening to Walt relate what had happened, the Chinese merchant stiffened in indignation and his black eyes glittered with resentment.

"You say this bomber man shot at you. Why?"

"He wanted to discourage me from coming any closer to him or the bomb, I suppose."

"Did you see his face?"

"No."

"But you think you hit him with a bullet as he ran away?"

"He broke stride and went down to one knee—that I clearly saw. When he ran on, he was limping badly."

Chen looked thoughtful. "If his wound is serious, he will seek medical attention. Most of the doctors in Portland have Chinese servants, who see all that is worth seeing and hear all that is worth hearing. The word will be spread among my people that a reward of twenty-five dollars will be paid to the person who gives the Sam Yup Company the name of this man. He must be found, tried, and punished."

"I agree. But let's leave that to the Portland police and the courts. The Chinese can't risk enforcing their concept of trial and punishment—no matter how great the justification."

"Such a thought would never enter our heads," Chen Yu said quietly, but his eyes were cold. "As you know, we are a law-abiding people."

He smiled as he rose and bowed. "Please, you will come now to my quarters, divest yourself of your soiled clothes, and permit my personal physician to examine your wounds. After he has treated you, a hot bath will be drawn, you will be made clean and relaxed by the hands of women skilled in these arts, and then we will enjoy our customary pleasant evening. . . ."

4

Like most of Portland's Chinese merchants, Chen Yu's quarters occupied the second floor of the building that housed his import company. In terms of space and furnishings, they were far more luxurious than the outward appearance of the building indicated. Few white men ever had been invited into the living and dining rooms, Walt knew, and until this evening he himself had not seen the large, spotlessly clean, tiled room in which male members of the household and privileged guests were given baths.

Heathen Chinese, indeed! Walt mused as he viewed the big, square pool. This would shame the bathing facilities of the finest Victorian home in Portland. And the personal service was—well, *damned* personal. But he did believe he could get used to it.

In addition to the doctor, who was thin, stooped, and elderly, three Chinese women were in the room. Two of them were young and very pretty; the other was mature and very businesslike. As they helped him out of his clothes, he wondered if the two girls were part of the recently arrived shipment of fifteen-year-old virgins. If so, the matron who was bossing them, and now and then impatiently doing a task herself when their inexperienced fingers fumbled at unfamiliar snaps and buttons, no doubt would make sure that the merchandise remained uninspected and undamaged until Sunday's auction.

While the doctor examined his injuries, he lay facedown on a woven straw mat—naked, mind you, *stark, jaybird naked—* wondering if the way he was feeling was the way a young virgin felt when on the auction block. Vulnerable, embarrassed, defenseless. *Oh, cruel, crass, heartless world! You see only my lovely body, not my soul. You will buy me, use me, then, when the bloom of my youth has gone, cast me aside.* . . .

An unexpected painful jab in the flesh of his right buttock ended Walt's reverie and brought him rudely back to reality. No, he could not imagine with any degree of authenticity how a fifteen-year-old virgin Chinese girl felt on the auction block. Among other drawbacks, he was male, American, and twenty-nine.

Though the pidgin English of the Chinese doctor was difficult to understand, Walt gathered that the injury to his left shoulder blade was a bruise, not a break, which would be sore for a few days but would heal without further attention. But the buttock wound, which had been made by a board with several "lusty nails" in it, required lancing, swabbing, and cauterizing, and must be watched closely, the doctor said, lest it "get inflected."

As he lay soaking and sipping a mild, low-proof whisky one of the girls brought him, he was intrigued by Chen Yu's prediction that if the bomber sought medical attention his identity would become known to the Chinese. What would happen then? Well, Chen Yu *could* tell Walt, who *could* go to the Portland police. When they asked him how he could positively identify the man as the bomber, he *could* say: "I put a bullet in him." To which the man no doubt would respond by denying everything, then would countercharge Walt with unprovoked assault with intent to kill.

No, that would not do at all. In these times, any white man who bore witness against his own race in favor of the Chinese risked ostracism, bodily harm, or worse. Still, there were several interesting things he could do with the information, when and if he learned the man's name. He could tip off an editor friend on the *Oregonian*, for example, whose questions would scare hell out of the bastard. He could make sure that the bomber learned that the Sam Yup Company had paid twenty-five dollars—a full month's wage for the average Chinese workingman—to learn his identity, and then let him sweat blood as he wondered what the Sam Yup Company intended doing with the information.

Right now in the Portland Chinese community a bitter struggle for power was going on between the Six Companies, which claimed to be benevolent societies, and the tongs, which were bands of Chinese criminals seeking to control business, labor, prostitution, and the drug trade by threats, extortion, and murder. Few Americans knew the difference between a benevolent-minded company and a murder-oriented tong.

"Hell, a Chinaman is a Chinaman!" said the white radicals. "Aren't they all alike?"

Being a violent man himself, the bomber no doubt would suspect the worst of the Sam Yup Company and would guess that it had put a price on his head. Since the favorite weapon of the *boy hoy doy*—a guild of hired Chinese assassins—was a lather's hatchet, which guild rules required always be left in the victim's skull, news that his identity was known and his name now posted in Sam Yup Company headquarters in Chinatown would cause the bomber some sleepless nights. Which would serve him right, because if anybody deserved—

"You finish hot bath now," the Chinese matron told Walt matter-of-factly. "You hop out, catchee warm towel, catchee slap-slap. Makee feel good."

Toweled dry by the two young girls, slapped, rubbed, and massaged by the matron, his buttock wound poulticed and dressed by the elderly doctor, and his glass refilled with sipping whisky, Walt indeed felt good as he slipped his feet into wooden clogs and his arms into the sleeves of a black silk robe. Mellow though he was, he must be firm with Chen about stopping the auction, he mused. He must explain to him in no uncertain terms that the law had to be obeyed. He must make it crystal clear that certain Chinese customs would not be tolerated in America.

Which was a shame, in a way. Because in his view, the ancient and honorable civilization of China had many worthy customs America would do well to adopt.

Its ancient and honorable mode of bathing, for instance . . .

5

Like a formal Chinese dinner in which innumerable dishes are served and guests take only a single bite of each, a serious conversation with Chen Yu required a great deal of time and yielded more savor than substance. While drinking, while eating, and while playing poker during the course of the long evening, Chen parried every inquiry Walt made about the slave girl auction, gave evasive answers to Inspector McClure's charge that the Sam Yup Company was importing Chinese girls for purposes of prostitution, and acted more like a cunning defense witness being questioned by a hostile prosecuting attorney than like a businessman client being advised by his own friendly lawyer.

The gist of Chen Yu's testimony, if condensed into a brief, would have read:

"The inspector is mistaken. My nephews are boys, not girls . . . unless a substitution has been made outside my knowledge . . . by a merchant, perhaps, who wishes a female companion. . . .

"Yes, in China such a woman is called a concubine. She may have been sold by her parents while yet a child for a few piculs of rice and trained to please men. Girl-children are of no worth, you see—except where scarce, as in America. . . .

"Is it not the market that makes the trade? Is it not good business to ship a commodity worth only one hundred dollars in Canton to America, where it is worth two or three thousand dollars . . . ?

"No, in our view this is not slavery. The girl wishes to better her lot. She has no skills except to please men. In exchange for her passage money, her food, and her lodging, she signs a contract with a broker to give her services for a term of four years. When she reaches America, employers seek her out and enter competitive bids. The winning bidder then places the money in her hands. . . .

"True, she does not keep the money. She passes it on to the agent of the company that sponsored her. It is not hers, you see, until she has completed the term of her employment. The company keeps it for her. . . ."

Whether the excitement, the drinks, or his growing sense of exasperation triggered his action, Walt did not know. But his patience suddenly reached its limits. Tossing in his cards, he got to his feet and said bluntly: "Enough, Chen. I quit."

"You concede the hand?"

"The hand, the evening, my job—the whole ball of wax. When a client won't listen to his attorney's advice, they'd better end their relationship."

Chen frowned. "I have offended you."

"You sure have."

"How?"

"By not listening to a word I say. By being dense and stubborn. In fact, Chen, you've got to be the stubbornest son of a bitch I've ever worked for."

For an instant, Chen Yu's dark eyes glittered dangerously, then his face broke into a smile. Inclining his head in a polite, submissive gesture, he motioned for Walt to sit down.

"In America, I have learned, friends may call each other the vilest of names and no offense is given or taken—if they are smiling. I am smiling, Walt. Are you?"

As he sat down, Walt's smile was weak, but it was a smile. "Sure I am, Chen. And I'm sorry for what I said."

"No, it is true. I am dense. I am stubborn. I pretend not to hear what I do not wish to be so." He beckoned to a young Chinese girl crouching in a shadowy corner of the room; she hastened to the table, poured their glasses full of whisky, then retired to her corner. Chen lifted his glass. "To a better understanding?"

"That I'll drink to."

They touched glasses and drank. After a silence, Chen said quietly, "It is difficult for me to comprehend why Inspector McClure, the Portland police, and you, as my attorney, have become so concerned over a matter that should not trouble you at all. But since you have, I shall do whatever you advise. Where do we begin?"

"With the truth. Is an auction of six young girls planned for Sunday afternoon?"

"Yes."

"You must cancel it."

"I shall—though reluctantly. It would have been both interesting and profitable."

"You must close all the red-light houses in Chinatown."

"Permanently?"

"No. But the Portland police can save a lot of face with the bluenoses if they can take credit for making the Chinese obey the law. They won't forget the favor."

Chen sighed. "Very well. Tomorrow they will be closed."

"Now about those six young girls. They can't just drop out of sight. Too many people know about them. We've got to do one of two things: let Inspector McClure arrest and deport them, or find a way to legalize their entry."

"I would prefer the latter alternative. You have experience in these matters. How much will it cost?"

"At a guess, I'll need five hundred dollars a girl," Walt said. "This will include my legal services."

Chen nodded. "Three thousand dollars is a great deal of money. But what must be paid, shall be paid."

"Money is only part of the solution. Each of those girls must move into a respectable household and become part of a family whose moral rectitude is above reproach. Ideally, she should appear to be a daughter or wife—"

"Pardon the interruption, but this expression 'moral rectitude' is new to me. What does it mean?"

"That the family doesn't misbehave in public and is wealthy enough to command respect."

"Ah yes! Just as in China! This can be arranged. In fact, the very merchants who would have been bidding on the girls no doubt can be persuaded—"

"No details, Chen," Walt cut in, holding up a silencing hand. "You see, after the papers are drawn up, I will be required to swear that the statements made in them are true and are backed up by documents mailed months ago in Canton but now unfortunately missing—"

"A most intriguing solution. What is the nature of these missing documents?"

"Proof that the girls have a legal right to leave China and join their father, husband, or husband-to-be in the United States, which person now resides in Portland and has registered under the Geary Act." Walt paused, frowning. "No, let's simplify that to husband-to-be. It will be much more convincing if the girls actually marry the merchants who take them in. That's the only arrangement American bluenoses will accept. Will your people agree?"

"If a Chinese merchant in Portland wished to marry a girl living in China," Chen answered, "he would do so by proxy before she left home. Without being married, she would never leave home—if she were a respectable girl. You understand this?"

"So far. Go on."

"No wealthy Chinese merchant in Portland would agree to marry one of these girls in a Chinese ceremony conducted here. However, if you are speaking of an American ceremony—"

"I am—the simplest kind: a license and a few words read by a J.P."

" 'Jay Pee'?"

"Justice of peace. In our court system, that's as low as you can get and still be an official. But a J.P. is an official. In fact, I'm one myself."

"Excellent! You can obtain the license, you can conduct the ceremony, and to my people it will have no validity whatso-

ever. Under these circumstances, I am sure they will coop-
erate." His smile returning, Chen Yu picked up the cards and
started shuffling. "Your luck has been very good tonight. Shall
we resume our game?"

6

So far as Walt Randall knew, there was no law that required an attorney to inform a client of the jokers written into a contract that the client had voluntarily agreed to sign, though most attorneys did take care to supply that information. But because he was about to become involved in a slight case of fraud on his client's behalf, because his throbbing, aching buttock was making him drink whisky faster and in greater quantity than he usually did, and because his pride had been rankled by Chen's remark that a ceremony conducted by Walt as a "Jay Pee" would have no validity whatsoever with the Chinese merchants, Walt did not trouble to point out a joker of some importance in the agreement just made. Which was that in Oregon a marriage performed by a J.P. was legally just as binding and morally just as inviolable as one consecrated in a church.

Sure, the rich merchants who would end up with the girls all had wives, children, and concubines back in China, for no Chinaman of means failed to return to his homeland at least once every five years. Unless he stayed in his native village at least a year on each visit, he lost face. Unless he acquired a wife on his first trip home and left the seed of a child with her then and on all subsequent trips, he became an object of scorn and contempt. Unless the business he had set up in the United States could be run by his employees—as few could—he must return to the land of *Gum Shan* eventually, of course, for how else could he make enough gold to support his family in China, buy more rice land, build a new house for his close relatives, rent the old house to more distant relatives, and make gifts with which to build schools and hospitals, to the glory of his name?

But what he did while sojourning in the United States mattered little to his family in China, as long as he made money and sent it home.

All right, Walt brooded as he emptied his glass and gingerly shifted his weight off the wounded buttock, *so I'll be an accessory to bigamy—on six counts.* Was such a crime listed in Oregon's criminal code? Since the state was founded by bluenoses, it probably was. But to his way of thinking, it shouldn't be. Any man fool enough to take on two or more wives deserved exactly what they would give him in the way of punishment—and the matter should end there.

"Aces and nines," Chen said, spreading his two pair faceup on the table. "Can you beat them?"

"Just barely," Walt said, laying down his own hand. "Three queens."

"You are lucky. Very lucky."

As Walt raked in the chips and shuffled the cards, Chen motioned again to the Chinese girl kneeling on a cushion in a shadowed corner of the room, and again she moved quickly to refill their glasses. Chen said something to her in Chinese; she hesitated, then reached out, placed the palm of her right hand against Walt's forehead, left it there for a second or two, then turned and touched Chen Yu's forehead in the same manner. Bowing and smiling to both men, she retired to her corner.

"What was that for?" Walt asked.

"She transferred good fortune from you to me. Did-you not feel the good luck spirit leave your head?"

"All my feelings right now are on the other end," Walt grunted as he extended the deck to be cut. He tossed two blue chips into the pot. "Just to see if she did swipe my luck, let's play another hand of draw."

Chen cut, Walt put the deck back together and, as he dealt, glanced at the girl.

"Isn't she a new one?"

"Yes."

"One of *them?*"

"Yes. In my opinion, probably the best of the lot, though of course men's tastes vary. It is difficult to predict which girl will bring the highest price."

"What's her name?"

"Ming Sen."

"She's pretty."

"Yes. She is also strong and healthy. I will have one card."

"Dealer takes two."

"Without looking, fifty dollars says I have hit my straight."

"You're covered. And raised fifty."

"Now, I'll look." Chen peered at his cards, smiled broadly, and picked up ten blue chips. "I'll see you—and say one hundred more."

Without hesitation, Walt covered the bet and spread his hand. It contained only a pair of jacks. Chen sighed and tossed in his cards. "How did you know I missed?"

"You overacted."

"In the future," Chen said solemnly, "I shall be inscrutable."

Walt took a couple of swallows of his drink. Probably it was just his imagination, but the spot on his forehead where the girl's hand had rested felt cool and relaxed while the rest of his face felt hot and tense. Probably it was just the whisky in him, but he could have sworn that she had tried to convey a message to him with her eyes. A plea for help? An appeal to be rescued?

Sure, just like in the romantic novels, Walt mused sardonically, *where the tender young virgin is saved from the clutches of a lecher three times her age by a young, clean-living hero with impeccable morals. . . .*

From the way she walked, her feet had never been bound. In China, this would mark her as a lowborn person, Walt knew, unfit to marry a merchant, an official, or a scholar; she could only become the wife of a farmer or laborer. Highborn women, who had had their feet bound and crippled into useless knots no more than four inches long, could walk only a few steps; yet they were cherished as brides. She could walk normally; so she was handicapped. How was that for topsy-turvy thinking?

Chen's stack of poker chips was getting low; he now had less than two hundred dollars' worth left. Reaching for the watch in his vest pocket to check the time, Walt became aware of the fact that he still was wearing the black silk robe. He also became aware that his glass was empty again and that Ming Sen had hastened forward to refill it. He blinked at Chen.

"What time is it?"

"Eleven o'clock."

"Whose deal is it?"

"Yours."

Two ways I can go, Walt brooded as he shuffled the cards. *I can carry him along for the next hour and let him save a little face. Or I can go for the bundle now, wipe him out, go home, and get off my aching butt. Give me a sign, cards. A weak hand, I carry him. A strong hand, I clobber him.*

He picked up his cards—the deuce of spades, the eight of hearts, and three kings. *Okay. I go for the bundle.*

Chen drew one card and Walt drew two. After they both had bet and raised, Chen shoved his last chip into the center of the table and Walt covered.

"This time I am not acting," Chen said, spreading his hand. "I did hit, you see. A queen-high straight." He smiled condescendingly. "What did your two-card draw give you to go with your three of a kind?"

"Just a pair of sixes," Walt said, laying down the full house. He shook his head sympathetically. "You were snakebit tonight, Chen."

With his well-groomed fingertips touching and his graceful hands placed on the table before him, the Chinese merchant sat for several moments in silence, his eyes closed. Then he reopened them and gazed intently at Walt.

"Your luck has been incredible. Would you play one more hand?"

"You're out of chips, Chen. You know our rules. We bet only what we bring to the table."

Raising a hand, Chen beckoned to Ming Sen, who hastened forward, refilled Walt's glass, and started to retire. Chen spoke sharply to her, she bowed submissively to him and to Walt, then stood gazing demurely down at the floor.

"I owe you twenty-five hundred dollars in gold," Chen said. "If the auction were held Sunday, Ming Sen would bring that amount—probably more. We will play one final hand, with the stakes to be what I owe you—against the girl. If I win, we are even. If you win, you take home both the gold and Ming Sen."

Walt took a long swallow of whisky, set the glass down, and smiled at Chen. "You've got to be joking."

"No. I am serious."

"She's a human being. Slavery is against the law."

"As I explained to you earlier, she has been taught how to please men—an honorable art—and has signed a contract agreeing to sell her services to the highest bidder for a term of four years. In our view, this does not make her a slave."

"All right, I'll concede that point. But I'm a bachelor with a boar's nest of an apartment across the hall from my office. I've got a houseboy, who keeps the place clean, cooks for me when I don't eat out, and keeps his mouth shut about my personal affairs. What would I do with her?"

"That is not for me to say," Chen murmured as he picked up the cards and riffled them. "But if you win her, I am sure you will think of something."

"If I win her, how will I explain her to my friends?"

"Many white families in Portland have Chinese servants," Chen said with a shrug. "What will there be to explain?"

"Well, for openers: she's a fifteen-year-old virgin; I kept her off the auction block; she's in the country illegally; and I won her in a poker game. That should start the conversational ball rolling."

"Among my people, it is considered bad manners to inquire about the personal relationship between members of a respectable household," Chen said, placing the deck on the table near Walt's hand. "It is assumed that if these people do not misbehave in public, their moral rectitude is above reproach. You will cut the deck, please?"

Walt looked again at the girl's face. At first glance, he had judged her beauty fragile and delicate, but now he saw a hint of strength and durability. She was no China doll. Her high cheekbones, her wide-set eyes, her broad-nostriled nose, and her generous mouth gave her face character, young though she was. Chen said something to her in Chinese. Her head lifted in perceptible pride, her eyes widened as she gazed directly at Walt, and a brief flash of spirit glinted in them.

"Does she speak English?" Walt asked.

"A little. And she learns very quickly."

"Could it be, Chen, that you've spent the whole evening setting me up for this?" Walt asked. "Could it be that you want to make sure I'm as deeply involved in this girl-importing business as you are? Could it be that you want to make sure we sink or swim together?"

"We Chinese are not as devious as we are made out to be," Chen said with a smile. "But we do have a tendency to lay the solving of our problems in the laps of the gods. Please, you will cut the cards?"

Walt reached for the deck.

7

On this lovely mid-March day, Walt Randall sat with his feet propped up on his desk gazing out the open casement windows of his office at the distant skyline. Call it lassitude. Call it contentment. Call it plain old laziness. By any name, it inclined him to vacillate rather than plan, to ignore problems rather than face them, to walk away from responsibility rather than accept it.

He sighed. Blame Ming Sen for his lack of energy. Ever since the night he had brought her home from the poker game, he had been living in a dream world, in which nothing that happened really mattered except the experiences they shared with each other. *She* was real enough. Oh, Lord, *was* she real! But their relationship was so lacking in moral, racial, or legal validity that he could not for one moment conceive it to be permanent. Already, as the two letters he had just received testified, pressures were building up to destroy it. Too soon, damn it! Too soon!

Dropping his feet to the floor, he picked up one of the letters and read it for the second time. It was from his brother, Allan, who, as always, was dreaming big.

> Dear Walt:
>
> Keep your fingers crossed for me, but I do believe I've found a live one this time. Farley Smythe—he insists I drop his title—thinks prospects for the Golden Girl "look jolly good." He's deposited a draft for $25,000 in a Lewiston bank to pay wages and expenses

for exploratory work and has recommended to his London office that $100,000 more be spent drilling a tunnel through the base of the ridge where I first struck the vein. So it looks like we're off and running.

It would be a big help, Walt, if you could plant a story in the *Oregonian* about a new mining boom in Hell's Canyon. Tell the paper a well-heeled British syndicate has sent an expert to Idaho to make sure they get first crack at it. You know how those things build up. Get me the right kind of puff in the *Oregonian* and I'll be able to sell ten dollars' worth of stock to the general public for every dollar the British syndicate puts up. "If the *Oregonian* prints a story," people say, "it must be true."

Not that this isn't true. The Golden Girl is the best prospect I've ever seen—and I've been in mining a long time. But it's going to be expensive to develop, so I'll need all the money I can get.

How much of a company do we have to organize before we can sell stock? I'd be obliged if you'd set it up. Cut yourself in for a liberal share and a spot on the Board of Directors. Have a lot of fancy-looking stock certificates printed.

Incidentally, one problem that worries Farley and me is where we're going to get the cheap labor we'll need to work the Golden Girl. What do you think of using Chinamen? Could you arrange it with that fellow you work for, Chen Yu? Or would using Chinese miners get us in trouble with the Workingmen's Party?

Speaking of Chen Yu, I hear you won a Chinese girl from him in a poker game. Tsk! Tsk! Tsk! Is it true what they say about them? Be careful you don't catch Yellow Jaundice! Ha! Ha! Ha!

Yours,

Allan

Walt winced at the crudeness of his brother's humor. Lewiston was three hundred and seventy miles upriver from Portland. Even so, the poker game story had reached Allan in less than two weeks, so it must now be common knowledge in business, legal, and social circles all over the Pacific Northwest.

It was easy to guess how the story had spread. At seven o'clock on the morning after the game, he had been rudely awakened by an ungodly clanging of pots and pans in the kitchen of his apartment, followed by a shrill cry of an oriental male in distress and a torrent of angry female scolding. Staggering out of bed, he had crossed the bedroom and dining room—painfully stubbing a toe en route—lurched against the frame of the kitchen door, and just managed to save himself from falling by grabbing and bracing himself against the door jamb.

"What in the hell is going on?" he shouted.

Wong, his Chinese houseboy, untangled himself from the clutter of kitchen utensils that had tumbled down off a shelf, which had collapsed as he tried to climb on top of it to escape the menacing meat cleaver in Ming Sen's hand. His face several shades paler than usual, he pointed a trembling finger at the girl and cried: "She no go! I tell her get out, she no go! She try choppee me head off!"

Waving the cleaver under the houseboy's nose, Ming Sen let loose another torrent of words. Walt groaned and closed his eyes. Friday having been Wong's night off, he had not been in the apartment when his master and newly won prize came home in a hansom cab, tripped up the stairs, and went to bed. Naturally enough, upon seeing Ming this morning, the houseboy assumed that she was overstaying the time and purpose for which she had been invited to the apartment and had ordered her to leave. Feeling insulted, she had taken immediate steps to correct his erroneous assumption regarding her status. The Chinese, Walt had learned, were very sensitive about status.

"It's all right, Wong," he said wearily. "She can stay—at least for a while."

"She say she belong you now."

"In a way, she does."

"She say she gonna boss this house. Boss kitchen, boss bedroom, boss me, boss every damn thing. You likee that?"

To the best of Walt's hazy remembrance, she was more than adequate as boss of the bedroom. Since she now was demonstrating how quickly she could take over the rest of the house, he saw no reason to object.

"Admit it, Wong—this is a boar's nest. Maybe a woman's touch is what it needs. Let's give her a try, shall we?"

Since he had no choice, Wong grudgingly agreed. But from that moment on, everything the new mistress did was relayed by the houseboy to his Chinese and white friends as he appealed to them for sympathy. Wong was spoiled, of course. The most envied job a Chinese servant could have was working for a well-to-do, generous, unmarried white man. Such a man invariably turned running the household and paying the bills over to his "boy"; thus, the prospects for squeeze were as large as the chores were small. So long as meals were served when wanted, beds were made when needed, clothes were kept in wearable shape, and no large piles of rubbish got in his way, a bachelor seldom complained.

But let a woman move in—particularly a Chinese woman— and the houseboy's days of ease were over. . . .

Walt sighed. Like most white men, Allan assumed that there could be only one aspect to a relationship between his brother and a Chinese girl. Like most white men, Allan had a dirty mind. *Well, they can all go to hell,* Walt mused. *It's no business of theirs.* Still, he was troubled by the fact that Ming Sen's presence in his household was so widely known, for these were explosive times.

He picked up the second letter, which had been delivered by a messenger from the headquarters of the Sam Yup Company. It was written and signed by Chen Yu:

Honorable Friend Mr. Walt Randall:

The party in question the night of the affair of the washhouse on 2nd Street is identified without question by the name Patrick O'Reilly, member of the Workingmen's Party, twice candidate for the Oregon Legislature, now editor of a weekly Radical publication called *The Torch*.

His wound is in the fleshy part of the upper left leg, where the bullet lodged against but did not break the bone. He now walks with a cane. Our informant secured said bullet from the operating pan of Dr. Luther Franklin, who removed it, without Dr. Franklin's knowledge. Said bullet is herewith returned to you for identification with your pistol.

For the time being, we shall take no action against Patrick O' Reilly, trusting in your good judgment to do what is best for the law-abiding Chinese of Portland, who wish only to be good citizens. . . .

Tossing the letter aside, Walt swore heartily. *God damn the contrariness of the Irish!* For every Jim McClure, who was a decent man, there had to be a Patrick O'Reilly, who was a rabble-rouser. The weekly publication piously called *The Torch*, whose masthead carried the symbol of liberty held aloft in a clenched fist, had as its slogan: *"The Chinese Must Go!"* It was a political paper, pure and simple, and its owner-publisher-editor, Patrick O'Reilly, was exploiting racial hatred at its vilest level to promote a bloc of votes in his third try for the Oregon Legislature.

As a result of the washhouse explosion, two Chinese laundrymen had died, another had lost an arm, and a child had been blinded. Yet in the next issue of *The Torch*, Patrick O'Reilly claimed that the Chinese themselves had set off the bomb in a maudlin appeal for sympathy, had miscalculated the length of its fuse, and had become the victims· of their own stupidity.

Walt Randall's face hardened. A man that heartless deserved a liberal dose of the very medicine he was trying to force on the Chinese—fear. Getting up from his desk, he buckled on his gunbelt and holstered Smith and Wesson, picked up the letter from Chen Yu, crossed the office and closed the door behind him. At the click of the latch, he heard the sound of feet padding quickly across the living room of his apartment on the far side of the landing, the door opened, and Ming Sen stood smiling at him.

"You finish work?"

"In the office, yes. But I've got to go out for a while."

"You come back soon?"

"One hour." He held up his right hand with its index finger extended. "Okay?"

"Okay!" she murmured. Laughing happily, she reached for his hands. He pulled her to him; she leaned her upper body away from him in mock terror, exclaiming, "Such big, strong man! You scare me much!"

He kissed her, then said gruffly, "Not as much as you scare me," and headed down the stairs.

8

When dealing with an editor as seasoned and cynical as Ray Pierce, the safest course was to tell him the simple truth, Walt had learned, and trust to his judgment as to how much or how little of it should be published. A ponderous, beetle-browed man with a massive shock of gray hair, Pierce wheeled around in his swivel chair as Walt Randall approached his desk in the *Oregonian* office, waved a copy-editing pencil at him like a band conductor's baton, and boomed: "Just the man I've been wanting to talk to! Sit down, Walt! Sit down!"

"What have I done now?" Walt asked warily, as he took a chair.

"Not you. Your brother, Allan. I got a letter from him this morning." Pawing through the disorderly pile of copy, clippings, and correspondence on his desk, Ray Pierce found the sheet he was looking for and scanned it through his steel-rimmed glasses. "He seems to think he's hit it big."

"He always does, Ray. For twenty years, every show of color he's found has been a potential bonanza. His hopes overwhelm his common sense."

"A perfect definition of a mining man," Pierce grunted. "But this time he's interested British capital."

"So I hear."

"Smythe spent a couple of weeks in Portland before he went upriver," Pierce said. "The questions he asked in mining circles made a lot of people suspicious, including me. So I did some checking by wire and cable with New York and London."

"What did you find out?"

"He's titled, wealthy, and financial adviser to one of the biggest international mining syndicates in the world. A favorable word from him could mean a substantial investment of British money in your brother's mine. So Allan really may have hit it big."

"For his sake, I hope so. He doesn't have much to show for all the years he's spent chasing rainbows."

"What do you know about the Golden Girl? Where's it located? Are there other prospects in the area? How does a person get there? Have you ever seen that part of the country?"

Walt sighed in resignation. Whether Allan's mine was a good prospect or not, the fact that a foreign syndicate was considering investing a substantial amount of money in it would be news of prime importance to the *Oregonian,* for every pound of freight and every dollar expended must pass through the Portland business community. The more Walt downplayed the prospect, the better it would look—a fact Allan no doubt had counted on.

"Yes, I've seen Hell's Canyon. In the deepest part, it's sixty-five hundred feet from water level up to the canyon's rim. The Golden Girl is on the Oregon side of the canyon, fifty-five miles upriver from Lewiston."

"Any roads to it?"

"No. Only pack trails. Even these are bad."

"Access by river?"

"Not on a regular basis. Above Lewiston, the Snake is a devil of a river, with rapids every mile or so. Allan owns a small stern-wheeler he's taken sixty or seventy miles up the Snake—but only in seasons of favorable water."

"How big a boat?"

"Fully loaded, she'll carry a hundred tons."

"Allan says you're forming a mining company and plan to sell shares to the public. He says you're to be a director."

Walt shook his head. "I don't plan to go into the mining business with my brother, though I will try to keep his operations legal. If the British syndicate does put up money, I imagine they'll insist on retaining control—say fifty-one per cent of the stock. Allowing Allan twenty per cent as discoverer and myself five per cent for the legal work involved, that would leave roughly one fourth of the shares to be offered to the public."

"Will this affect your relationship with Chen Yu?"

"In no way. As a matter of fact, it's because of Chen that I came in to see you."

"What's his problem?"

"He's given me the name of the man who bombed the Chinese washhouse a couple of weeks ago."

"Who?"

"Patrick O'Reilly."

"The loudmouthed Irishman who publishes *The Torch?*"

"The same."

"Why, that hypocritical son of a bitch! What kind of proof does Chen have?"

Walt told him.

"Have you taken this to the police?"

"Not yet. I wanted to talk to you first."

Removing his glasses, the newspaperman leaned back in his chair, polished the lenses with a none too clean handkerchief, peered at the glasses against the light, then grunted, "Spell it out, Walt. What kind of help do you need?"

"Two innocent Chinese laundrymen were killed by that bomb, Ray. Another lost an arm. A six-year-old boy was blinded for life. Why? So a rabble-rousing politician can build race hatred into a bloc of votes. Such a man should be exposed—and if possible sent to prison."

The editor's gaze dropped to the holstered Smith and Wesson on Walt's right hip. "Since when did you start wearing a gun in daylight?"

"Since the night of the bombing. As Chen Yu's attorney, I've been threatened a number of times by the radicals. Patrick O'Reilly himself took a shot at me."

"And you shot back," Pierce grunted. "Too bad it was only his leg you hit."

"The light was poor. Next time I'll try to do better."

"You want O'Reilly exposed, you say. In print?"

"Yes."

"Normally, evidence goes from the police to the prosecuting attorney, who passes it on to a grand jury. After considering it in secret, the grand jury issues an indictment—if the jurors in their collective wisdom feel a crime has been committed. Why not go that route?"

"Because the chief of police and the prosecutor are politically in hock to the Workingmen's Party. Unless your paper supports me, I'll never get a hearing convened."

"Have you any indication from Chen Yu that the Chinese are considering taking justice into their own hands?"

"I've warned him against that, Ray. They're patient, law-abiding people. But push them too far—"

"I know!" Ray Pierce said grimly. "Up until now, Portland is one of the few cities in the West that hasn't had a riot. With no false modesty, I credit the *Oregonian*'s firm stand in favor of law and order for that."

"All I'm asking is that you maintain that stand."

"We'll support you, Walt," Pierce said with a nod. "But you know what's at stake?"

"O'Reilly's political career. His freedom. Maybe even his life. His friends in the Workingmen's Party won't take his exposure lightly."

"And you'll be their target."

"I'll take that risk."

"All right," Pierce said curtly, making notes on a piece of paper. "Here's the way we'll go at it. Give me a copy of every piece of evidence you turn over to the police: your statement, Chen's statement, the statement of Dr. Luther Franklin and his Chinese servant. Better give me the bullet, too—these things have a way of disappearing around police stations. Get me the names of the dead and injured Chinese, with as much family background on them as possible. I'll have an artist make a sketch of the laundryman who lost an arm and the boy who was blinded. We'll run the sketches on the front page, with the story. Damn it, Walt, I want our readers to understand that these are *people* who are being maimed and killed."

"I'll get it to you by dark," Walt said with a nod. "The same information will go to the chief of police tomorrow morning."

"Good! It will be set up in type when you put it in his hand —and the paper will be on the street two hours later. Tell him that, Walt."

"I will."

"You can also tell him if he doesn't take action on this, I'll have his hide. We're going to have law and order in Portland, by God, if I have to skin every official in the city!"

9

By noon, next day, Walt knew that his accusation and the *Oregonian*'s demand that justice be done were being heatedly discussed all over Portland. Devoting its entire front page to the story, the newspaper had shown in detailed pen-and-ink sketches the maimed Chinese laundryman and the blinded boy. Both were well known to the white community, for they were father and son, habitually making rounds together in a one-horse wagon picking up and delivering clothes.

In summing up the reaction of "the overwhelming majority of Portland's decent citizens to this despicable act by a cowardly man attempting to promote his political ambitions . . ." the paper quoted a Methodist minister's wife, a women's rights leader, and an elderly missionary just returned from China:

> "Sheer barbarity!"
> "Outrageous!"
> "Inhuman!"

In a front-page editorial, Ray Pierce asked four pointed questions:

HOW LONG?????

> Will we tolerate bigotry . . . ?
> Listen to hate-peddlers . . . ?
> Let murder go unpunished . . . ?
> Leave inept officials in office . . . ?

Lunching with the editor in the dining room of the Willamette Hotel, whose well-dressed, well-mannered patrons bore little resemblance to the radical leaders of the Workingmen's Party, Walt accepted the nods, back-pats, and handshakes of business and professional men for what they were: approval of a principle, law and order, which they hoped he and the *Oregonian* editor could make the police and the prosecuting attorney enforce.

Chortling with glee, Ray Pierce unfolded several scraps of paper he had taken out of a coat pocket and read them aloud:

"'The police don't play no favorites,' Chief Abe Browder declared firmly when questioned by a reporter. 'Now that this evidence has been placed in my hands, I'm turning it over to the prosecutor's office immediately. I'm ready and willing to make an arrest the minute he gives me the word. . . .'"

"'I am shocked that a man of Patrick O'Reilly's standing should appear to be involved in such a terrible crime,' Prosecutor Wesley Cameron said solemnly. 'A grand jury will be convened tomorrow morning. You may rest assured, sir, that my office will take prompt action to implement its verdict. However, may I say that since a person is presumed innocent until found guilty, I deplore the fact that your paper chose to publicize the evidence against Mr. O'Reilly in such a sensational manner. This office would have carried out its duties with or without the *Oregonian*'s support. . . .'"

With a snort of disgust, Ray Pierce took a healthy swallow of his whisky and water. He laughed. "In a pig's eye, it would! It hasn't prosecuted a white man for doing violence to the Chinese since Wesley Cameron has been in office."

"He is right about one thing. We are sensationalizing the charges against O'Reilly."

"You're damned right we are. But only because he used his own paper to sensationalize lies designed to stir up the rabble." The editor pawed through the scraps of paper. "We've got a beautiful batch of quotes from O'Reilly himself. Simply beautiful! First, he claimed he was nowhere near the wash-house that night. He said his pistol went off while he was cleaning it. Then he changed his story and claimed a stray bullet from a saloon brawl nicked him as he walked along the street in another part of town. Finally, he claimed he heard the firebell ring while eating supper, ran to join the volunteers, and was shot by a man lurking in the shadows. . . ."

"Meaning me. He'll claim next that I planted the bomb and shot him when he discovered me in the act."

"No doubt he will. But he won't be believed by anybody that counts."

Going back to his office, Walt spent the mild spring afternoon writing a letter to his brother, Allan, outlining what must be done to set up a stock-mining company and the pitfalls to be avoided in order to keep the operation legal. Probably it was a waste of time, for Allan had been pursuing his dream of treasure far too long to be amenable to reason, logic, or legality. Like others of his kind, he had developed a pet theory as to where precious metals were to be found, and he expounded it beautifully. Once the initial premise of that theory was accepted—and Allan himself had been the first person *to* accept it—the inexorable correctness of its conclusion could not be denied.

Reduced to its simplest terms, Allan's theory was that since precious metals were formed in the molten bowels of the earth, they surfaced most profusely in regions where the earth's crust had ruptured most violently. Nowhere in North America had such intense geologic violence occurred as in the depths of Hell's Canyon. Therefore, this area must contain the richest deposits of treasure in the entire continent.

Because of its inaccessibility, few white prospectors had gone into the canyon, so its potential insofar as precious metals was concerned was largely unknown. Flour gold depos-

ited by eddies on sandbars by the seasonal rise and fall of the
river had been found in numerous spots, but the time, patience, and labor required to pan three to five dollars a day
made such diggings unappealing to white men. These sandbars were worked by the ubiquitous Chinese, groups of whom
somehow made their way to the remotest, most difficult to
reach coves in the depths of the canyon in the summer each
year when the river subsided, stayed through the winter and
spring, and then moved out as the early summer rise covered
the sandbars.

Like other white men, Allan had no interest in flour gold.
His ceaseless search had been for a surface outcropping that
would indicate a vein leading through the basaltic overlay
into granite and the mother lode itself. It was there some-
place. It *had* to be there! Now at long last he appeared to have
found it.

Weary of writing, Walt Randall lay aside his pen, crossed
the room, and stood gazing out the window at Mount Hood,
whose eleven-thousand-foot snow-clad peak showed vividly
clear in the late afternoon sunlight despite the fact that it was
over forty miles away. It would greatly simplify matters, he
mused, if he took a couple of weeks off, went upriver to Lewiston, and conferred with Allan and Farley Smythe now that
they had returned from their inspection trip to the Golden
Girl.

Once Patrick O'Reilly was indicted—as he surely would be—
his defense attorney would ask for and get at least sixty days
to prepare his defense. Two weeks' absence from Portland on
Walt's part would give the hotheads in the Workingmen's
Party time to cool off. And spring came early to Lewiston.

Starting to turn away from the window, he paused as shouts
came from the boardwalk across the street.

"Hey, Randall—you up there?"

"Chink lover! Stick your head out the window!"

"Yeah, you bastard! Let us see your pigtails!"

Three roughly dressed men stood below, shaking fists and
making obscene gestures. One of them was groping in the

muddy street, attempting to mold wet earth and horse manure into a ball solid enough to throw. Walt leaned out the window and waved genially.

"Gentlemen, you honor me."

The man making the missile stood up, drew back his arm, and threw it. Disintegrating in mid-flight, it fell to the ground short of its target. The man himself stumbled and would have fallen on his face had he not been caught by his arms by his two companions.

"Show us your slave girl, Randall!"

"Yeah—we might want to buy some of that!"

"What'll you rent her out for—a dollar a screw?"

From directly below, out of Walt's range of vision, an authoritative voice cried: "That'll be enough out of yez! Move along, boys! Move along, I say!"

"Aw, go soak your head in a rain barrel," the missile thrower muttered. "This is a free country, ain't it?"

"That it is, bully boy," said Kevin Coughlin, the burly, red-faced policeman who patrolled daytime on this beat. "And it's myself'll be feelin' free to give you a thumpin' on your hard Mick head if you don't move on and quit disturbin' the peace. Move on, I say!"

Sullenly the three men sauntered off, making obscene gestures up at Walt but being careful to do nothing that would give Patrolman Coughlin offense. He was known to be a very tough cop.

"Sure, and if I were you, Mr. Randall," he called up, "I'd close those windows and drapes."

"I like the fresh air, Kevin."

"There's talk against you by the radicals, sir. Wild talk. I go off duty at dark. It's then trouble will come, I'm thinkin'."

"If it does, I'll be ready for it."

"Close the windows, sir, draw the drapes, and show no light that can be seen from the street—that's my advice. Good luck, Mr. Randall."

"Thanks, Kevin."

With the coming of darkness, Walt took the officer's advice, closing the windows, drawing the drapes, going down the stairs and bolting the street door from the inside. Drops of moisture glistened on the outside glass surface of the small, square, iron-grilled window in the upper panel of the door; a typical Oregon mist whose droplets were too fine to be called rain was beginning to fall, as it did so often this time of year. Or any time of year, he mused disgustedly as he struck a match, turned up the gas jet of the vestibule lamp, and lighted it.

Climbing the stairs and going into his living quarters across the hall from his office, he recalled the clear, sunny days, the cloudless, star-studded nights, and the fabulous fishing he and his brother had enjoyed during a week-long trip into the lower reaches of Hell's Canyon about this time last year.

Lord almighty! It will be good to wet a line again! That's the tonic I need to flush out the poisons of a long, gray, rainy winter. . . .

Before Ming Sen joined the household, Walt and the houseboy Wong had gotten along well enough in an easygoing sort of way. Grudgingly, Wong would lay a fire, turn up the reading lamp, fetch the evening paper, mix a drink, help Walt out of his muddy boots, and fix a meal, when requested to do so. But he liked to be shouted at when given an order, for this gave him the right to grumble about how abused he was and scold Walt for being such a demanding employer who did not appreciate what a jewel of a houseboy he had. Till recently, it had been a comfortable relationship. But Ming's coming had altered it drastically.

This evening as he came into the living room Walt did not have to shout: "Hey, Wong, you lazy rascal! How about—"

For the fire was burning, the reading lamp was turned up, his carpet slippers, footstool, and evening paper were exactly where they should be, and Ming Sen, freshly bathed and beautifully groomed, was running across the room to kiss him and help him out of his coat.

"Boots off? Jacket? Drinkee?"

"In that order," Walt said with a smile, putting his arm

around her as he moved toward the leather chair facing the fire. "Lord, you smell good!"

Laughing self-consciously, she knelt and took hold of a boot. Despite her slender build, she was surprisingly strong. Carrying his boots out to the kitchen, she issued a sharp order in Cantonese to Wong. The houseboy gave a squeal of protest. Ming had ordered him to clean and shine the boots, Walt knew, and they *would* be cleaned and shined. But Wong was unhappy because he no longer could complain directly to the master of the household.

When Ming Sen returned to the living room, she was carrying Walt's smoking jacket and a lightly watered glass of whisky. She sank down on the floor beside his chair, her feet folded under her, her face lifted, her dark, almond-shaped eyes searching his for a sign that she pleased him.

Out of curiosity, Walt had asked Chen Yu if he knew anything about her background. Chen shook his head.

"In these matters, we deal with an agent in Canton. We do not require details of ancestry."

"Surely you know her clan."

"Yes. They are boat people. Lowborn, of course, but sturdy, durable, and very skilled on water." Chen looked at him quizzically. "Does she displease you in any way?"

Stroking the girl's shoulder, Walt sighed and took a sip of his drink. He was not displeased with Ming Sen. What displeased him was that the wily oriental merchant had involved him far more deeply than he cared to be involved in a delicate, explosive matter. The other five young virgins had been married in simple ceremonies to prominent Chinese merchants in Portland. But Chen Yu, instead of doing his duty as he had promised Walt he would, neatly had sidestepped it and delivered the sixth girl to Walt's bed and board.

Obviously, the present situation could not continue indefinitely. He would have a talk with Chen soon, Walt decided. He would tell the merchant quite firmly that he must take Ming back. Quite firmly, indeed.

Tomorrow, perhaps.

Or certainly next week. . . .

10

Someone had hold of his shoulder and was shaking him. His aftersupper nap not yet finished, he resisted coming awake, keeping his eyes closed and refusing to return to full consciousness. From a distance he could hear a roaring—like that of surf on a stormy coast, rapids in a narrow canyon of a swift-flowing river, a crowd cheering a speaker at a political rally. Nearer, words were being exchanged between Wong and Ming Sen in sharp, alarmed Cantonese. And Ming was pestering him with unwonted rudeness.

"Come awake, Mistah Walt! You come awake quick!"

"Go 'way."

"Big buncha men, Mistah Walt. Bad men. You wake up come see!"

Drowsily Walt opened his eyes. He recalled having two drinks, eating supper, then sitting down before the fire to read the evening paper. He recalled feeling full and content. He recalled closing his eyes to rest them for a moment or two. But he must have slept at least half an hour, for the mantel clock said eight-thirty.

Wong was standing at the living-room window, parting the heavy folds of the gold-colored drapes just enough to let him peer down at the street without himself being seen from below. Fully awake now, Walt patted Ming's hand reassuringly, then called to the houseboy.

"What's happening, Wong?"

"Lotsa men raise hell. Lotsa dlunks. Lotsa talk-talk all same like before 'lection."

Crossing the room, Walt thrust Wong aside, pushed back

the drapes and stared down at the street. It was filled with roughly dressed men, who, from the way they jostled, staggered, pushed, and clung to one another certainly were drunk. Their gestures and cries were directed at the windows of Walt's living quarters.

"To hell with the Chinese!"

"To hell with Chink lovers!"

"To hell with Walt Randall! Come on out, you bastard, and face us like a man!"

"Burn him out!"

"Yeah! Put the torch to his damned rat's nest!"

Scattered through the crowd, half a dozen pine knot torches flickered fitfully in the fine-dropped falling rain, which had soaked the frame building to such an extent that fire was no danger unless an incendiary aid such as kerosene was used. The mob of men below looked and behaved like rabble; undirected, gutless, and incapable of maintaining coherence or cohesiveness long enough between drinks to plan or do any damage. Even so, Walt did not intend to endure the mob's presence outside the entrance to his home indefinitely. Nor did he wish to risk the safety of the two Orientals now sheltered by his roof.

"Make trouble, you think?" Wong asked anxiously.

"Probably all they'll make is noise," Walt muttered. "But just to be on the safe side, you and Ming had better leave and go to the Chinese quarter. Take the back stairs down to the alley—"

"Mistah Walt—" Ming said at his elbow.

"Yes?"

"You want gun, yes? You shoot Irish bastards, like before."

Surprised both by what she had said and the tone of her voice as she said it, Walt turned and stared at the Chinese girl. She was holding the gunbelt and holstered revolver, which he customarily hung on a coatrack just inside the living-room door. Taking the gunbelt, he buckled it around his waist.

"You learn fast, Ming." He put his hands on her shoulders.

"Listen to me. This is no place for you. Wong will take you to Chen Yu's house—"

"No."

"Yes." Walt looked at Wong. "Tell Chen it's too dangerous having her stay here. Tell him that he must be personally responsible for her from now on. Tell him I'll come see him tomorrow and we'll talk about what must be done."

"No!" Ming exclaimed. "No!"

From the street came a wave of angry shouting; glass tinkled as an empty bottle struck a window pane and shattered it. Wong seized Ming by the arm.

"Come on—we go!"

Lashing out at the houseboy in a torrent of impassioned Cantonese, Ming jerked her arm out of his grasp, backed across the room to the fireplace, snatched up an iron poker, then moved toward Wong, brandishing it menacingly. Wong sought refuge behind his master.

"Mistah Walt, she stubborn bitch. She say this her home now. She say she belong you. She say she lose face if she leave you."

"All right, she can stay for a while," Walt said impatiently. "But you get to Chen Yu as fast as you can. Tell him to send over a couple of his strong-arm boys, with orders to pack her off to the Chinese quarter."

"Will do."

"Ming, go lock the back stairs door behind Wong after he leaves. Put down that poker, for God's sake. You're scaring Wong to death."

Arguing in whispers, the houseboy and the Chinese girl headed for the rear of the living quarters, where an outside staircase off the kitchen led to the alley below. Walt turned down the living-room lamps so that the window giving on the street was in darkness. Another missile—this one a brick—came crashing through a pane of glass, followed by a drunken cheer from the crowd.

"Enough of *that*," Walt murmured, opened the window frame just enough to insert the barrel of the Smith and Wesson, took careful aim at a torch held by a man standing on the opposite boardwalk, and fired. At the roar of the revolver, the torch went spinning to the ground. Shouts of dismay went up from the crowd.

"He's got a gun!"

"He's shootin' at us!"

"Faith, an' I got no stomach for this!"

In the silence that had suddenly fallen over the crowd, Walt shouted, "Faith, and none of you have guts enough to do more than rant and rave and swill whisky. Get back to the saloon, bully boys! Haven't you sense enough to come in out of the rain?"

Grumbling and muttering imprecations, the crowd began to move back out of range. Shouting insults at a dark, inanimate upstairs window was a game men fortified with a half-hour supply of liquid courage didn't mind playing. Making themselves targets to a man defending his home with a gun from behind that window was a sport none cared to engage in.

But even as the mob was about to disperse, it stopped moving as a shout went up.

"Here he comes!"

"Patrick O'Reilly himself!"

"Now, by God, we'll see some action!"

Flanked by two men carrying torches, Patrick O'Reilly, editor of *The Torch*, guardian of such precious American freedoms as the right to drive all Chinese immigrants back where the yellow devils came from, champion of the Workingmen's Party, and perennial candidate for political office, came limping down the street. In his left hand, he carried a cane. In his right hand, he held an object whose identity Walt could not make out. Listening to the cheers that greeted the editor's appearance, watching the way the crowd parted to let O'Reilly through as the man limped purposefully to a position in the middle of the street just below the window, Walt mused: *He's staged this scene cleverly. How well will he play it?*

Lifting his head, O'Reilly called: "Walt Randall! Are you up there?"

"Yes," Walt answered curtly, pushing back the drapes and opening the casement window. "I'm here."

"You have slandered me, sir. I've come to inform you that I am filing a suit against you for one hundred thousand dollars."

"It's past office hours, O'Reilly. But if you'll serve the papers on me tomorrow, I'll respond in proper form."

"I'm going to break you, Randall. I'm going to show you up for the whore-mongering, Chink-loving, un-American son of a bitch you are. I'm going to destroy you and that ring of Chinese devils you work for, with your slave auctions, opium smoking, and all the other abominations you have brought into this country—"

"From a prison cell, you're going to do all this—after you're convicted of arson and murder?"

"Lies, Randall!" the editor shouted angrily, with the crowd roaring its vocal support. "*Your* lies—which I'll have no trouble disproving." Shaking the object held in his right hand, which Walt now recognized as a short-stocked whip with a coiled leather lash, O'Reilly cried, "Come down here, Randall! I'm going to horsewhip you within an inch of your life!"

Gazing down at the crowd of men, the flickering torches, the editor, and the falling rain, Walt smiled. *Not a badly played scene. Melodramatic. Overdone. But well suited to its audience.*

"*Bravo!*" Walt called down. "Great show! You should book it into every barroom in town! But if you don't mind, I'll wait to see you perform it in court."

The farce should have ended there; in fact, Walt guessed from the way Patrick O'Reilly turned away, that the editor fully intended to say and do no more. But applause is a heady thing to an actor or a politician. The cheers of the crowd tempted the editor to ad-lib one last movement and line. As the tumult died down, he turned back toward the window, shook the horsewhip, and cried: "Coward! Do I have to drag you into the street to get my satisfaction?"

"That's the ticket!" a man in the crowd shouted.

"Bust down the door!"

"Drag him down the stairs!"

"We're behind you, Pat!"

Galvanized into sudden movement, the mob of men seethed across the street toward the door, carrying Patrick O'Reilly before them like a wood chip on the crest of a wave. Solid though the door was, Walt knew it could not withstand for very long the battering it was getting. Running across the living room, he stepped out onto the upstairs landing, drew the revolver, and waited, staring down. Ming Sen appeared. He waved her away.

"Stay out of this, hear me?"

Below, the street door was being attacked with a pine-knot torch swung like a sledge hammer. A panel splintered. A hand reached in, seized the bolt, and slid it aside. A voice shouted: "It's open! Go get him, Pat!"

O'Reilly appeared in the vestibule below. He had a pistol in his right hand and was peering up the stairway, looking and no doubt feeling uncomfortable, for his body was a clearly defined target in the entryway gaslight while Walt could be seen only vaguely on the stair landing above.

"You're overplaying your part, O'Reilly," Walt called. "Get out before you get hurt."

"Like hell, I will!" the editor cried, his voice shrill with panic. "Take this!"

Flame blossomed. A stinging blow in the upper part of Walt's left leg told him he had been hit. He fired the Smith and Wesson. O'Reilly's body jerked as he spun half around, then the editor laughed crazily, hysterically, and started climbing the stairs, firing as he came.

My God, he's a madman! Walt thought. *It's him or me.* He raised the pistol to fire again.

A hammer blow struck him in the left chest. Sagging to his knees, reaching out for support, he was vaguely aware that Ming Sen had run out onto the landing. She was trying to hold him erect. The pistol had become a dead weight in his right hand. As it fell to the floor, she reached out and seized it, turned, and aimed it down the stairs.

"No," Walt murmured. "No. . ."

Another shot slammed up from below, this one catching Walt in his right shoulder. As consciousness began to leave him, he got a brief, vivid picture of Ming Sen firing down the stairs, once, twice, and yet a third time. Patrick O'Reilly, half-way up, straightened, made a gurgling sound, then went tumbling down the stairs to the vestibule.

In the long silence, a whimpering voice below breathed: "Holy Mother of Christ! Right in the face!"

Walt Randall knew no more. . . .

Crouched on the upstairs landing, Ming Sen cradled Walt's head in her lap, waiting for she knew not what. Violence was nothing new to her; she was familiar with raids made by murderous river pirates who came to one's houseboat in the night to plunder and kill. While prudence normally required a person to run, to hide, to evade trouble any way you could, when your home was invaded, you had to stand and fight. This was her home. She had killed to defend it—and would kill again, if any other member of the mob supporting the man she had shot ventured up the stairs.

None did so. Apprehensively gazing up, a man kneeling beside the body in the vestibule called: "Don't shoot no more, Randall—this ain't our quarrel. We've sent for the police ambulance. For God's sake, don't shoot no more!"

Concerned for her master, Ming dragged him into the living room, turned up the lamps, and examined his wounds. The one in his left leg and the one in his right shoulder were bleeding profusely; the one in the upper part of his left chest was hardly bleeding at all, but she judged it to be the most serious, for the bullet that caused it had penetrated the chest cavity.

Going into the bedroom, she took a clean white sheet out of a bureau drawer, got a pair of scissors, returned to the living room and quickly cut pads for bandages and strips with which to hold them in place. As she worked, she heard the wailing rise and fall of the hand-turned siren on the police ambulance, the clatter of hoofs, the rattle of wheels, the piercing blast of whistles, then the voices of officers asking questions and the gabble of men making replies. Hearing steps moving up the stairs, she remembered the pistol she had left lying on the landing. Knotting a bandage strip tight, she scurried out to the landing, picked up the gun, and aimed it at the blue-coated man halfway up the stairs. Squinting into the shadows, he paused.

"Randall—that you?"

"Mistah Walt get shot. Hurt bad."

"You his Chinese girl?"

"Yes. Me Ming Sen."

"Is that a gun you're holding?"

"Yes. Belong Mistah Randall."

"Take it easy, Ming—I'm not going to hurt you. Just be careful with that gun. You understand what I'm saying?"

"Yes."

"Put it down—gently."

"Yes. Now you come see Mistah Walt? Him hurt bad."

The policeman moved up the stairs, picked up the pistol with a grunt of relief, then followed her into the living room, where he bent over her master and examined him carefully. Shaking his head, he straightened, went to the landing, and called down: "Doc, we need you up here. Randall is in bad shape."

"O'Reilly is dead."

"Figured he was. Come on up and see if you can do anything for Randall."

Limited though her knowledge of English was, Ming Sen understood enough of the exchange between the policeman and the doctor who had come up the stairs and was now examining her master to realize that they were his friends. She was also aware that they were talking about her.

"This the slave girl Randall won from Chen Yu?"

"Yeah."

"We should be so lucky."

"She didn't bring Randall luck."

"Damn fool to keep her. Still, if I were twenty years younger and a bachelor . . ."

"Think you can save him?"

"He's got three bullets in him that I've got to dig out," the doctor said, shaking his head. "He's lost a lot of blood and he's in deep shock. Anytime you operate under those conditions, the odds are stacked against you. But I'll give it a try." Patting Ming's hand, which had seized his arm in panic at his headshake, the doctor gave her a reassuring smile and murmured, "I'll give it a damn good try."

11

Breathing heavily after his climb up the stairs, United States Customs and Immigration Inspector James McClure rapped on the door of Walt Randall's living quarters. When Ming Sen opened it, he took off his hat and said, "Afternoon, Ming. How's he doing today?"

"He is better. Much better."

"All right for me to talk to him?"

"You are his friend. He will be glad to see you. Please come in."

Scowling as he thought of the unhappy duty that faced him, Inspector McClure followed the slim, shapely Chinese girl as she led him to the bedroom where Walt Randall lay recuperating from his wounds. It had been a terrible ordeal for him, Inspector McClure knew—the pain, the infection, the fever, the long weeks when his life hung by a thread. Though the best medical men in Portland had worked long and diligently to save him, the deciding factor in his recovery, McClure had been told by the police surgeon, had been Ming Sen's nursing care.

Hour after hour, day after day, night after night, she had stayed at his side, tending to his needs with skilled, fierce devotion. When his chest wound became infected and failed to respond to conventional treatment by white doctors, it had been she who sent for Chen Yu's personal physician, she who applied the poultices of spider's web, bread mold, and other nauseous substances prescribed by the Chinese doctor, she who went to the apothecary shop in the Chinese quarter and ordered mixtures and tinctures of oriental roots, dried plant leaves, and herbs, she who had forced her master to drink the horrible-tasting medicine.

"God knows what's in the stuff," the police surgeon had told McClure. "But it seems to do the work."

No question about it. Walt Randall owed a great deal to Ming Sen. But the bureaucratic heat on Inspector McClure had become more than he could bear. Now he faced the unpleasant task of telling Walt he must get rid of her. . . .

Walt stared at him bleakly. "She saved my life, Mac."

"I know. You couldn't have had a better nurse."

"She did more than nurse me. During the gunfight, she—" Walt broke off. "Or did she tell you about that?"

"Never mind what she told me," Inspector McClure said gruffly. "All I know is what went into the grand jury record."

"Which was—?"

"A mob of men led by Patrick O'Reilly threatened you and broke down your door. During an exchange of shots between you and the deceased—he having fired first—you killed him in justifiable self-defense."

"Leave it at that." Walt scowled, then said, "I agree Ming has to go. The question is where?"

"I can serve illegal entry papers on her and deport her to China. She's probably got relatives there."

"She'd never be allowed to go back to them. As the property of the agent who bought her and shipped her to America, she'd be put in a brothel."

"Chen arranged marriages for the other girls. Can't he do the same for her?"

Gazing out the window, where scattered white clouds floated in a balmy blue April sky, Walt realized that the decision he long had postponed must be made now. Because of her age and race, Ming Sen could not lead a respectable life in this country without a husband to protect her. Because of her notoriety as the Chinese slave girl won in a poker game, no decent white family in Portland would hire her as a servant. Since she was no longer a virgin, her market value in the

Chinese community no doubt had decreased, though Chen Yu probably could peddle her to a middle-class Chinese trades- man.

If Walt himself attempted to marry her—and he had thought long and seriously about that possibility—the union would not be legal because of Oregon's miscegenation law, which prohibited marriage between a white American and "a member of an inferior race. . . ."

Sure, he could say to hell with the law. He and Ming could live together as man and wife, as they had been doing these past two months, with little likelihood that they would be arrested and thrown in jail. But he knew all too well what such an extralegal union would do to his career. It would end it, so far as patronage from white clients was concerned. With the anti-Chinese tide still rising in a nation beset by hard times, unemployment, and racial bigotry, it was highly proba- ble that Orientals residing in the United States eventually would be dispossessed and expelled from the country.

If that happened, how could he protect Ming? Assuming they started a family, how could he protect their children, which by law would be illegitimate? With Chen Yu impover- ished and deported and no white law practice, how could he make a living as an attorney?

There was one other thing that must be considered. With Patrick O'Reilly dead and the Workingmen's Party tempo- rarily leaderless, the feeling against the Chinese in Portland had simmered down to discontented grumblings among the ranks of the unemployed. But this was too potent a political issue to die for lack of a demagogue to espouse it. Sooner or later, Walt knew, another politically ambitious radical would appear and attempt to rally the unwashed masses behind him.

So long as Ming lived with Walt, so long as she remained visible as a beautiful Chinese girl in a white bachelor house- hold, so long as the possibility existed that it might become known that she, not Walt, had killed Patrick O'Reilly, making the deceased editor of *The Torch* a martyr to his cause—the tinder for a potentially destructive explosion would be present. The risk was too great to take.

Turning away from the window, Walt nodded to Inspector McClure. "All right, Mac. I'll ask Chen Yu to come see me tomorrow."

In response to the message hand-carried to him by the houseboy, Wong, the Chinese merchant wrote that he "would be happy to pay my good friend Honorable Mister Walt Randall a call tomorrow afternoon at five o'clock. . . ."

With Ming assisting him, Walt got out of bed, put on slippers and a robe, and managed to limp into the living room, where he sat down in his leather armchair. Receiving Chen Yu while reclining in bed would have been bad manners, for it would have implied a helplessness that he no longer felt. And the time had come when he must demonstrate to Ming that he no longer needed her as a nurse.

Last night, he had tried to tell her why she must leave. She had not understood. She simply had looked at him, smiled, shook her head, and said, "No leave, Mistah Walt. Belong you. Love you. No leave."

Damn it, why did she have to say such stupid things? Slavery was illegal in America. And what did she know about love? He had never mentioned the subject himself. Sure, he was fond of her. If the law permitted, he would have had no objection to marrying her. But since such a marriage *was* illegal, since getting her out of this household *was* for her own good, why wouldn't she listen to reason? Why had her comprehension of English suddenly deteriorated to the point that no matter what he said, she simply smiled, shook her head, and murmured, "No leave, Mistah Walt. No leave."

Worn out from his fruitless efforts to make her understand, he had fallen asleep with her sitting beside the bed holding his hand. His last waking thought had been: *The hell with it— let Chen Yu tell her. . . .*

Promptly at five o'clock, the Chinese merchant rapped on

the door. Standing beside Walt's chair, composed and radiant, Ming Sen waited while Wong hastened to open it.

Wong bowed to Chen. Ming bowed to him. The Chinese merchant approached Walt's chair, bowed, then impulsively reached out and clasped Walt's right hand between both of his.

"I'm delighted to see you making a recovery."

"Thank you, Chen. Your health is good?"

"Excellent."

"Please sit down. Tea or whisky?"

"Whisky, please, very lightly touched with water."

"Same for me, Ming."

When she and the houseboy had left the room, Walt violated the usual leisurely oriental pace of doing business and went directly to the point.

"Inspector McClure came to see me yesterday. He says Ming has to go."

"He threatens to deport her?"

Walt nodded. "I talked him into accepting the same arrangement that was made for the other girls. But it's got to be done soon."

"Can you get along without her?"

"With Wong here, yes. She won't let him come near me as long as she's around. But now that I'm out of bed, he's all the help I need."

"Loyalty is a virtue of her clan," Chen said. "Have you told her she must go?"

"I've tried—but I can't seem to make her understand. Maybe you can explain it to her."

"Explanations are useless to a woman of her class," Chen said coldly. "But she will do as she is told. Chinese women always do."

Do they, really? Walt wondered as Ming Sen returned to the living room and served the drinks. Or was their meekness and apparent humility merely another surface form of behavior used on certain occasions—such as when company came—while an entirely different kind of behavior obtained for everyday living? Certainly Ming had managed to make the two men of this household toe the line when she put her will to it. And Walt suspected that if given more time she would have become even more independent of male domination.

"You want me to go now?" Ming asked.

"If you don't mind," Walt said.

Bowing, she backed out of the room.

"Well, Chen, what can you do for her?" Walt asked.

"None of the Portland merchants will take her now," Chen said, shaking his head. "They would lose face."

"She must be provided for. Well provided."

"Your concern for her future is commendable. But opportunities to place her are limited. Perhaps an establishment where men are entertained—?"

"I won't let you put her in a whorehouse, Chen. You must give me your word that you won't even consider that."

"You have it," Chen said with a sigh. He took a sip of his drink, then said thoughtfully, "Perhaps Ah Fat would take her."

"Who is he?"

"He is headman of a party of Chinese workmen who hire out to do labor requiring both strength and skill. They are clansmen from the Punyu district, near Canton."

"Boat people?"

"No. Land people. But Ming Sen will have no trouble understanding their dialect. And her knowledge of English will be useful."

"Are they new to the country?"

"They have been building railroad in central Oregon for the past two years. Now they are laid off. But we will find other work for them to do."

"What kind of man is Ah Fat?"

"Strong. Dependable. A man respected by both his employers and the men who work under him."

"In other words, a good foreman."

Chen nodded. "At present, there are ten men besides himself in his work party. Given two days' notice, they are prepared to go wherever the work is, furnishing their own tools, housing, and food. They will work long hours, stay sober, and never strike. Ah Fat guarantees that."

"For what kind of pay?"

"This varies according to the nature of the work. But as an average on construction projects, it runs two dollars and fifty cents a day per man."

That was fifty cents more a day than labor customarily was paid in this part of the country, Walt knew, which refuted the claim made by members of the Workingmen's Party that the Chinese were undercutting wage rates. Of course when an employer hired a white laborer, whether he be Irish, Italian, Polish, Swedish, or just plain mongrelized American, arrangements must be made to feed and house him when he was away from home, the employer must constantly replenish vanishing tools, must expect a high rate of absenteeism following each payday, and must run the risk of job-crippling strikes. No wonder the Chinese could ask and get a premium wage.

"Would Ah Fat marry Ming and treat her with respect?"

"He is a dependable man," Chen answered, nodding. "If he says he will do a thing, it will be done."

"Have a talk with him, then. If he agrees, tell him to come here tomorrow morning at ten. I'll try to prepare Ming for it."

"She will obey me without question. Do you wish me to tell her?"

Walt hesitated, then nodded. "I'd appreciate it if you would. But gently, Chen. Very gently."

Finishing his drink, Chen Yu set down the empty glass and called out Ming's name. She came into the room, paused, and bowed to him. He spoke sharply to her in Chinese. She stiffened, gave Walt the briefest of glances, then moved forward and stood before Chen Yu, her head lowered, her eyes fixed on the floor. As the Chinese merchant continued speaking to her, Walt saw her face turn pale. She sank to one knee, nodding her head in a weak, helpless gesture of assent to Chen's final sharp question. He rose and smiled at Walt.

"It is done. She will marry Ah Fat and leave your household."

"Goddam it, Chen, I said gently. You just gave her an order."

"As I told you, one does not explain such matters to a woman. One simply tells her what he wants done." He bowed. "Now I shall take my leave. Ah Fat will be here tomorrow morning at ten o'clock."

Avoiding Walt's eyes, Ming Sen straightened, saw Chen Yu to the door, and closed it after him. Turning, she looked at Walt—simply looked—a hurt in her eyes that made him feel like the lowest bastard on earth.

Hell, it's for her own good, Walt told himself. *She'll get over it in time. And in time I'll forget the way she looked at me. A long, long time . . .*

"Help me back to bed, Ming," he said curtly. "I'm feeling a little tired. . . ."

How much of the proposed ceremony Ah Fat understood, Walt had no way of knowing, for the headman's only response to the questions asked of him had been a quickly muttered: "Yes, I do."

Several inches taller than the average Chinaman, he had a broad chest, powerful arms, and strong-looking, calloused hands. He appeared to be about thirty years old, had a broad face with unusually high cheekbones, and carried himself with the confidence of a person used to bossing men. Though obviously on his best behavior this morning, he now and again got a glint in his eyes as he glanced sideways at Ming that made Walt suspect him of having a brutal streak in his nature.

Oh, hell, who am I to worry about that? After the raw deal I gave her, the next man she gets can't possibly treat her any worse. But I've got to do all I can to protect her.

"After I have filled out this marriage certificate," Walt said, tapping the paper before him, "by the laws of this country, you and Ah Fat will be legally united. Do you understand that, Ming?"

"Yes. He will be my husband."

"Do you understand, Ah Fat?"

"Yes. She will be my wife."

"Make sure you treat her well. Because if you don't, the law will come after you, arrest you, and—"

He's laughing at me, Walt thought. *Though there isn't a sign of it on his face, I know that inside he's busting a gut laughing. But for Ming's sake, I've got to try and scare the bastard.*

Making a vertical chopping gesture with his right hand, Walt concluded: "Chop off your head. Now, if you're ready, we'll get on with the ceremony. Ah Fat, do you take this woman—"

"No!" Ming murmured in sudden anguish. "No, Mistah Walt, no!"

"It's for your own good, Ming. I've tried to explain that."

"No! Please, no!"

"Chen Yu told you—"

"No, Mistah Walt! Love you—not Ah Fat!"

Seizing Ming's upper arm in a grip so strong that she involuntarily cried out in pain, Ah Fat spat out a Chinese phrase so contemptuous that it needed no translation. Weak as he was, Walt lurched up out of his chair and moved toward him.

"You son of a bitch! Let go of her!"

Ah Fat released her arm and backed away, his manner obsequious and humble. "Sorry. Me no understand. Chen say marry. You say marry. She say marry. So I say marry. But now she say—"

"There's not going to be any marriage. Get out!"

"Sure, Mistah Randall! Whatever you say. I go quick."

Backing across the room to the door, Ah Fat opened it, scuttled out, slammed it shut, and went hurrying down the stairs. Horror-stricken by what she had done, Ming stood staring at Walt for several moments, her eyes filled with fear.

"Oh, Mistah Walt!" she exclaimed. "I have disgraced myself and dishonored you!"

"The hell you have!" he said huskily, opening his arms. "Come here!"

Whimpering, she ran to him and clung to him, her body shaking uncontrollably.

"Love you, Mistah Walt! Love you . . . !"

12

Normally, Inspector James McClure preferred dealing with Portland's Chinese community through an intermediary such as Walt Randall, who could engage in the bargaining procedures so beloved by oriental minds without involving the Customs and Immigration Bureau in open evasions of the law. But since Walt himself was one of the principals in the present embarrassing situation, Inspector McClure had no choice now but to confer directly with Chen Yu.

"As I see it, Chen, we're between a rock and a hard place," he told the Chinese merchant over a late afternoon drink in the importer's office. "Ming Sen is the scandal of Portland. She's made Randall take leave of his senses. She's made me nearly lose my job. And she's making a fool of you."

"In China, this could not happen," Chen said stiffly. "In China, women do as they are told."

"Yeah, but this ain't China. This is the United States of America, where the wind blows free and gives people all kinds of crazy notions. Ming Sen is a fast learner."

"With a good teacher. Can we not leave her with him?"

McClure shook his head. "Out of the question. After all the notoriety she's been given, every prune-faced female in town is prowling past Randall's place, hoping to get a squint at her. When she goes shopping with Wong, a regular parade of gawkers follows her. When she and Walt go out for a buggy ride, she dresses up like a princess, he puts the top down so he can show her off, and they act just like they were married."

"What is the harm in that?"

"None, so far as I'm concerned. But miscegenation is

against the law in Oregon. The bluenoses are up in arms. I can't take the heat I'm getting any longer."

"What do you plan to do—arrest Ming and deport her?"

"That's where things get complicated," McClure said uncomfortably, nodding assent as Chen moved to refill his glass. "In the first place, I promised Walt I wouldn't deport her. In the second place, arresting her for illegal entry would involve you as her sponsor—"

"Mistakes happen," Chen said. "I will admit a mistake was made, pay a fine, and let you deport her. That will end the matter."

"Not if Walt Randall raises a fuss."

"What can he do?"

"For openers, he can claim you've been importing girls for the purpose of prostitution for years. He can claim I've been a party to it. What's more, he can find a lot of people who will believe him."

"He is my attorney, Inspector McClure, paid to protect my interests, not injure them. He is your friend, indebted to you for many favors."

"He's also in love—for the first time in his life."

"So much so that he would replace his friendship for us, which pays him very well, with his loyalty to her, which pays him nothing?"

"She saved his life, Chen. He owes her for that."

Chen looked troubled. "What you are saying is that his love for her transcends his friendship with us. You are saying that if you attempt to deport her, he will make a public protest that will damage us both severely. Therefore, you are saying, she must be removed from his household and from public view in a manner so discreet that he cannot prove we had anything to do with it."

"Yeah, that's what I'm trying to say," McClure grunted. "But you've said it much better." Finishing his drink, he shook his head to a freshener, put down his glass, and rose to his feet. "Any ideas?"

"Yes," Chen said, also rising.

"No rough stuff, hear? Anybody harms that girl, they'll answer to me as well as him."

"She will not be hurt. You have my promise. She will leave his household of her own free will, drop out of sight, and will never be seen in Portland again. But she will not be hurt."

"Good. Make it soon."

Now that the weather had turned warm, fresh vegetables, wild mushrooms, seafood, and other perishables were being brought in daily to the tiny stalls of the Chinese quarter open-air market. Ming liked to do her food shopping there right after breakfast each morning, while selections were still at their best. Complaining as much as he dared, Wong went along, carrying the basket in which her purchases were placed, disagreeing with her on quality and price more frequently than the stall-keepers did, dawdling behind to exchange gossip with houseboy friends, then reappearing just in time to store her latest purchase in his basket, with a grin on his face, the smell of rice wine on his breath, and a flimsy excuse of having misunderstood her intentions as to which stall she had intended to visit next.

Halfway through her shopping tour this morning, Wong disappeared again. Since she had just purchased two pounds of fresh smelt—a small, delicious, oily fish of which Mistah Walt was very fond—and did not want to carry the leaky paper package in which the stall-keeper was wrapping the smelt in her bare hands while she searched for Wong, she became extremely exasperated. Seeing him through a break in the crowd, she moved away from the stall, calling in Cantonese: "Wong! Lazy, worthless son of a donkey, come here at once!"

Though he saw her, he did not obey her summons. Instead, he cast a quick, furtive glance in her direction, wheeled around, and vanished into the crowd. Before she could catch him and give him the dressing down he deserved, two tall, muscular Chinese men moved in on her, one from either side.

Hands closed on her upper arms, their grasp just firm enough to hold her immobile without causing her pain.

"You are Ming Sen?" one of the men said.

"Yes."

"Chen Yu wishes to see you. Come with us."

She had no choice, she knew, for these stern, black-clad men were employed by the elders of the Sam Yup Company to enforce orders made by the ruling council. Resistance would be useless. Still, if she screamed, held back, and compelled them to use force, they would lose face—just as she would lose face if they did not respect her person.

"I will come with you. But only if you let go of me."

They released her arms. She moved quietly with them, then, through the stalls of the market, up the street, through the busy aisles of the Chen Yu Importing Company store, and finally into the private office where the Chinese merchant sat behind his desk going over his books. Without a word, the two men bowed and withdrew, closing the door behind them. After a time, Chen Yu raised his head and gazed at her. His eyes were as cold as ice.

"Your presence in Walt Randall's household has become an embarrassment to the Chinese community."

"Three months ago, you told me to go there. I obeyed."

"I know. Last week, I told you to leave. You disobeyed."

"Mistah Walt did not want me to leave. So I stayed."

"Ah Fat told me what happened. You begged, you wheedled, you whined shamelessly. Ah Fat said you sounded like an unweaned pup being taken from its mother. Walt Randall is a kind-hearted man. He felt sorry for you and let you stay."

"He loves me. He has told me so."

"Perhaps he thinks he does. But I suspect all he feels for you is gratitude and pity."

"Whatever he feels, I must stay," Ming murmured, bowing her head. "For I know I love him."

"Your loyalty to him during his time of need was highly commendable," Chen Yu said. "But now you are doing him great harm by staying in his household."

"How?"

"You have become the symbol of a relationship greatly feared by Americans—the mixing of the white and yellow races. By law, you cannot marry. So you must not live together."

"Who do we harm by living together?"

"You make the entire Chinese community in Portland lose face. You endanger my good relations with Inspector McClure. Most important of all, you risk injuring Walt Randall himself, whose career as an attorney surely will be destroyed if you continue to live with him. For all these reasons, you must leave him."

"You order me to do this?"

"No. I ask you to do it of your own free will."

"When?"

"Immediately."

"How will I tell him?"

"By letter. I will bring in a secretary to whom you will dictate a letter in English, telling Walt Randall in your own words why you are leaving him and what you are going to do."

"What am I going to do?"

"Exactly what you agreed to do a week ago—marry Ah Fat in an American civil ceremony, then go away from Portland with him and his work crew to a place yet to be decided."

Raising her head, Ming said brokenly, "This is what I must do?"

"Yes, Ming, it is," Chen Yu said gently. "It will be difficult, I know. But, believe me, it will be best for all concerned. . . ."

For the past few days, Walt Randall had spent a couple of hours each morning working in his office, returning to his quarters across the hall for the noon meal and a long nap, then coming back to the office again in the afternoon and working two hours more. At four o'clock, if the day was sunny, Ming and Wong would help him down the stairs and into the buggy, which he would drive for an hour or so for a change of scene and a breath of fresh air. Daily, he was growing stronger; he hoped to be working full time in two or three weeks.

Today at noon, Ming Sen did not come to his office and tell him that lunch was ready, as she usually did. Puzzled, he took his watch out of his vest pocket, noted that it read twenty minutes past twelve, got up from his desk, and crossed the hall to his apartment. Entering it, he closed the door behind him.

"Ming!"

She did not answer. Hearing a noise in the kitchen, he limped in that direction. As he crossed the dining room, he called again, "Ming! Where in the devil are you?"

In the kitchen, Wong stood at the stove, vigorously stirring the contents of a boiling pot. The stiffness of his back and the fact that he did not turn around made Walt suspect that something was wrong.

"Wong, have you gone deaf?" Walt demanded angrily.

"Oh, no—me hear good," the houseboy said with a nervous giggle, hastily glancing over his shoulder at his master, then turning his attention back to the pot. "But you call for Ming, not for me."

"Sure, I want Ming, goddam it! Where is she?"

"Gone. Since early this morning, she gone."

"Where? Why? When is she coming back?"

"Don't know. But letter come for you by Sam Yup Company messenger boy half hour ago. You find it on table in living room. Maybeso it tell you something."

"Why in the hell did the messenger boy give it to you instead of bringing it to me in my office?"

"No savvy, Mistah Walt. He just bring it and go."

Limping into the living room, Walt picked up the envelope, tore it open, and read its brief, neatly penned message. At first, it failed to register. Then a sick feeling hit him in the pit of the stomach, his knees suddenly felt rubbery, and he sank into his leather chair with a groan.

"Ming—you couldn't!"

But she had. Not willingly, in all probability, but she had left him. She had married Ah Fat, become a part of the Chinese community, and had put herself forever out of reach so far as Walt was concerned. Shaking with helpless rage, he started to rise and go into the kitchen, found his legs too weak to support him, and sank back into his chair.

"Wong!" he cried angrily. "Come here, you sneaky bastard!"

After several moments, the houseboy padded timidly into the living room, pausing several steps away, poised for instant flight.

"You call me, Mistah Walt?"

"You knew about this, didn't you?"

"No, no! Me know nothing!"

"When did you see her last?"

"When we go to market light after bleakfast."

"Did you see Chen Yu's strong-arm boys grab her?"

"Me see nothing. Me know nothing. Honest-to-God, Mistah Walt, me don't know why she leave." Though his face retained its look of innocence, he could not keep a hint of glee out of his voice. "You think maybeso she don't come back?"

"You know she's not coming back," Walt said harshly. "And if I thought for a minute that you had anything to do with her leaving I'd boot your butt up between your ears."

Wong grinned joyously, for he had not been addressed in such familiar terms since Ming Sen had joined the household. "Lunch is leady. You want to eat now?"

"What I want is a drink," Walt muttered. "A stiff one."

"Coming up, chop-chop."

Crumpling envelope and letter into a ball, Walt threw it at the fireplace, leaned back in his chair, and closed his eyes. Goddam it, he should have anticipated this! When Jim McClure or Chen Yu made a promise, they kept it. They had a right to expect him to keep his. When he had reneged, telling Ah Fat to get out and Ming Sen to stay, they could have considered the bargain broken. McClure could have arrested

Ming and started deportation procedures. Chen Yu could have denounced her, paid a fine, and sent her back to China and life in a brothel. But they had not done so.

Why hadn't they? Probably because they suspected that Walt would raise holy hell with them, throwing every legal brickbat he could lay hands on at them. Would he have done such a thing? Taking the drink Wong brought him, gulping it down, then impatiently gesturing for the houseboy to bring him another, Walt brooded morosely: *Bet your sweet ass I would have! Bargain be damned!*

By keeping their side of the deal to the letter, they left him with no legal brickbats to throw. He could not attack Jim McClure, for the immigration officer had done nothing. It would be useless to accuse Chen Yu of kidnapping Ming, even if he had done so, for no Chinese witness would dare testify against him. Legally, Ah Fat and Ming were married now; the secretary Ming had dictated her letter to had thoughtfully noted the name of the justice of peace who had performed the ceremony and the hour at which it had taken place. Finding her in the Chinese quarter would be impossible without Chen Yu's help, and that he would never get.

Sure, he could give in to his gut impulse to act rashly and dramatically. He could bolt down the stairs two at a time, run across town to the Chinese quarter, burst into Chen's office, grab him by the throat, shake him till his teeth rattled, and tell him to bring Ming back or else. Or else what? Good question. The shape he was in, he would need Wong's help even to get *down* the stairs, let alone do any running, bursting, grabbing, and shaking.

But he could sit and drink. He sure as hell could do that! Bitterly he raised his glass in a mock toast.

"Chen, you clever son of a bitch, here's to you. First you gave her to me, then you took her away. It's all for the best, I know. But I'll hate you for it the rest of my life. . . ."

13

All factors considered, Chen Yu judged the project suggested by Ah Fat to be the best that had been proposed. It would require three boats, each capable of carrying four people, their provisions, tools, and shelter materials. Since the Columbia River east of Portland alternated stretches of quiet water with powerful rapids, oars would be needed for the slackwater sections, towlines for the rapids. At the two major portages—the Cascades and The Dalles—upriver passage for boats and people could be purchased on the steam-drawn railway cars. This would be expensive, but since labor usually was in short supply handling freight transferred from the river steamers, it would be possible for Ah Fat's party to work out their fares.

Because of the temper of the times, the party must stick together; Chen had cautioned Ah Fat about that. Whether panning gold in some newly deserted white mining camp, chopping wood for the boilers of the stern-wheelers, moving earth for roads, tending gardens, doing laundry, carrying water, or whatever the members of the party found to do, they must live together quietly, making their presence as inconspicuous as possible to the white community.

Their names were on record with the Sam Yup Company, the benevolent society that had paid their passage from Canton to Portland, supplied them with enough money to support themselves until they found work, guaranteed their passage home when they had made their stake, or would see to it that their bones were returned for burial in their homeland, should they die in America.

Before filing the list in his fireproof safe, Chen checked the names on it again: Kong Ngan, Kong Mun Kow, Chea Lin Chung, Chea Chow, Chea Ling, Chea Cheong, Chea Sun, Chea Yow, Chea Shun, and Chea Po. The headman, of course, was Ah Fat. Also included in the party was the girl, Ming Sen.

Chen frowned. Under ordinary circumstances, he would not have sent a lone girl—particularly one as young, pretty, and valuable as Ming was—with a work party into the interior of the country, where living conditions would be harsh and primitive. She would be much more comfortable—and financially much more productive—in a big-city brothel. But he had given Walt Randall his word. True, Walt had temporarily made it difficult for him to keep his word, but he had soon found a way to surmount the obstacle.

Chen sighed. Poor Walt! He had taken Ming's leaving very badly. For the time being, their relationship was strained. But sooner or later Walt would have to admit that getting Ming Sen out of Portland had been the wise thing to do. Still, the waste of marketable merchandise was regrettable.

Closing the file, he crossed the room and placed it in his safe. . . .

Walt's brother, Allan, had come downriver to Portland twice since the night of the shooting. Since he had been deeply drugged and irrational with fever, Walt remembered little of Allan's first visit. But during his second, when it became apparent that Walt was on the road to recovery, they had agreed that as soon as he was able to travel he would go upriver to Lewiston and spend what was left of the spring and summer recuperating his health and strength in the balmy climate that prevailed along the Snake River.

A week after Ming Sen left the household and married Ah Fat, Allan showed up unannounced. Bounding up the stairs with his usual exuberance, he burst into the office, where Walt was going through some papers, and exclaimed, "Hey, look at you! Up and about!"

"Barely," Walt said. Delighted to see his brother, he fended off an affectionate bear hug and shook Allan's hand. "But still tender in spots."

"You're thin as a rail and pale as a ghost. Well, I've got the cure for that!"

"How are things with you?"

"Booming like you wouldn't believe!"

Listening to his brother's account of what he and Lord Farley Windham Smythe had accomplished during the past two months, Walt found his feelings toward the mining venture changing from a cool skepticism to a warming interest. After making a careful inspection of several test holes on the site of the Golden Girl, Farley Smythe had agreed with Allan that their first step should be the drilling of a horizontal tunnel through the base of a basaltic spur near the spot where the Imnaha River flowed into the Snake. The British syndicate that he represented already had cabled a draft for $100,000 to a Portland bank, with which to pay workmen's wages and buy explosives, tools, and other needed supplies. An additional $100,000 credit had been approved for the purchase of a stamp mill, its size depending on what kind of equipment was available in the West and the practicality of transporting it to the difficult-to-reach site.

"It's a bitch of a place to work," Allan said. "Every man, tool, and pound of blasting powder has to be taken fifty-five miles upriver from Lewiston on my boat. There's a rapid for every mile—half a dozen of them killers. Where we're drilling, there's no horizontal space at all—everything's up and down. So we have to build foot room as we go."

"What are you using for labor?"

"To begin with, we took whatever we could pick up in Lewiston saloons and flophouses—out-of-luck prospectors, drunks, bums. We'd get two decent days work out of them in exchange for their grub, transportation upriver, and a week's pay, then they would quit or become so worthless we'd have to fire them."

"Sounds like expensive labor."

"It was. But Farley soon changed that. He took a trip up to

the Coeur d'Alene mines in northern Idaho, where they've got some immigrant Welsh miners working, and paid one of them premium wages to sign on with us as superintendent. Jesus, you should see him move rock! We've got half a dozen Irishmen who work well enough when they're sober—and get their butts kicked out of camp by the Welsh super when they get drunk. We've got five Chinese, who are real good help once they catch on to what we want them to do. The rest of the crew is a hodgepodge of drifters that come and go."

"What are you doing in Portland?"

"Lining up equipment. We've tunneled three hundred feet into the mountain and are about to lay narrow-gauge track for the ore cars we'll be using to haul rock out of the tunnel. They'll be pulled by mules. I've arranged for a ten-stamp mill to be shipped up from San Francisco."

"Are you into high-grade ore?"

"I had lunch with Ray Pierce," Allan said evasively, running a hand over his iron gray, still thick, still curly hair, "and answered a lot of his questions. I told him the Golden Girl still hasn't proved itself. Sure, the syndicate has put a couple of hundred thousand dollars into it. And the first sample of ore we shipped down to San Francisco did assay eight hundred dollars a ton. But like I told Ray—it was hand-sorted. We'll be lucky if run-of-the-vein ore goes two hundred. Of course with an estimated milling cost of eighty dollars a ton, that's not too bad."

"You're a wonder, Allan!" Walt said in amazement and exasperation. "You really are! What else did you reluctantly tell Ray Pierce, with the firm expectation that it will make headlines in tomorrow's *Oregonian?*"

"Not much," Allan answered with a grin. "Except that the syndicate is considering extending the Golden Girl's credit another $300,000." He paused. "I also mentioned that $500,000 worth of Golden Girl stock will be offered to the public as soon as we've filed the necessary papers."

"Did you find an attorney in Lewiston to do your legal work?"

"No. But I hired a printer to turn out a batch of stock certificates for me. Beautiful stuff! The shares are selling like hotcakes at ten bucks apiece."

Walt scowled at his brother. "Wait a minute! Are you telling me that without doing any legal work whatsoever, you're already selling shares in the Golden Girl?"

"Just to a few special friends, Walt. You know how it is. The word spreads you're into a good thing. Men you've known and done business with for years come to you with money in their hot, grubby hands, begging to be let in on the ground floor. So you do them a favor—"

"For God's sake, Allan, you can't operate a venture this big out of your hat. How much stock have you sold?"

"Oh, not much. Enough to pay travel expenses, that's all."

"How much?" Walt demanded grimly.

"Twenty, thirty—well, maybe fifty thousand dollars' worth."

Walt groaned. "With that kind of money, you can travel a long way—and may have to."

"Speaking of traveling," Allan said amiably, "do you feel like going back to Lewiston with me now? I'll set you up in an office there and you can start doing whatever legal work needs to be done."

"I'm well enough to travel, Allan. But I'm not sure I want to get involved with the Golden Girl—or with you. The way you're operating, you're a good bet for prison, being tarred and feathered, or hung."

"In which case, I'll need the best lawyer I can hire—which happens to be you," Allan said with a grin. His face sobered. "Ray Pierce tells me the Chinese girl left you."

"Yes," Walt said, tight-lipped.

"Ray says you thought a lot of her."

"She saved my life, Allan. I thought more of her than of any woman I've ever known. Please don't mention her again."

"If that's the way you want it, Walt."

An uncomfortable silence lay between them for several moments, then Walt said, "When do we leave?"

"Tomorrow morning. I've booked passage for us to the Cascades on the *Wide West*, with a first-class cabin off the dining room in case you want to lie down and rest. We'll take the *Hassalo* to The Dalles, where I've reserved the best room in the Umatilla House. You can have your supper served in bed, if you like. From Celilo Landing, we'll be aboard the newest boat on the upper river, the *Annie Faxon*. In the executive stateroom, no less."

"You go first-class, don't you, Allan?" Walt said, giving his older brother an affectionate smile.

"Why not?" Allan said with a shrug. "Since I'm going to be a millionaire, I might as well learn how to live like one."

14

Among the boat people of South China's Pearl River Delta, into whose clan Ming Sen had been born, durability and a kinship with water were the two basic qualities needed for survival. She had learned to swim before she learned to walk. Living on her father's boat until she was twelve years old, she had become as skilled at swimming, diving, and boat handling as he and his five sons were, and almost as strong. Lamenting the fact that she had not been born a boy-child, her poverty-stricken father had been forced to sell her, of course, as she approached womanhood, to an agent who supplied con-cubines and prostitutes to wealthy Chinese merchants in the land of *Gum Shan.*

"Soon our sons will marry and bring their wives home to live with us," he told her mother. "We will not have room for a girl-child. The price the agent offers is good. She will have plenty to eat, a comfortable place to live, and, if she is fortu-nate, a master who will not treat her too badly. This is the best we can do for her."

If her father or mother shed any tears over parting with their only daughter, they did not let Ming see them. Nor did she let them see hers. For three years, she was well housed, clothed, and fed as she underwent rigorous training in the art of pleasing men. Since dancing and vigorous physical exercise were part of that training, her muscles did not go soft. Though her opportunities to swim were more limited than when living on her father's boat, swimming, once learned, is a skill never forgotten. So bearing a full share of the labor and danger of moving the three rowboats upriver—which she was expected to do—proved no great burden to her.

Because she knew that if Ah Fat so desired he could turn her into a low-caste prostitute and make money on her by selling her services to the ten laborers in the party, she utilized all her feminine skills to please him and make him regard her as his personal property. In this, she succeeded, for he was a possessive, jealous man, who felt that he was very lucky to have acquired such a pretty, talented young woman, who, under ordinary circumstances, would have entered concubinage in the household of a wealthy merchant far above Ah Fat's station in life. Thus, the headman quickly made it clear to the laborers in the party that Ming Sen was exclusively his woman, to be shared with no one.

For this, Ming was grateful. Braiding her hair like a man, wearing the clothes of a man, keeping her voice low when encountering whites, as Ah Fat ordered her to do, she did her best to maintain the appearance of being but another member of an all-male party. Obeying his every command with a meekness and humility that gave him no cause to treat her with the brutality she knew he was capable of, she behaved as untold generations of Chinese women before her had done, acting out the old proverb: *"The green reed bends in the slightest breeze, but the typhoon does not break it."*

For the present, she accepted what she could not change. But the three months she had lived with Walt Randall had given her a knowledge of what life could be when a woman was respected and loved. She had been given a taste of American-style freedom unknown to women in her homeland; though she might never achieve it again, she would remember that period of freedom for the rest of her life.

Being land people, the laborers of the party were so inept and clumsy on water that Ming Sen, watching the first boat pull away from the Portland dock, squealed with laughter.

"Look at the dolts!" she cried to Ah Fat, pointing at the floundering crew. "The way they use the oars, they look like they are chopping wood or flailing grain rather than rowing a boat!"

"Can you teach them to do better?" the headman demanded angrily.

"Certainly. Tell them to come back to the dock. I will show them how to get twice the results with half the effort."

When the boat and the four clansmen returned to the landing, Ming gave them a lesson in water lore. It was not necessary for all four of them to face forward, she said, wielding only one oar as if paddling a canoe, thrusting it deep into the water as if digging a hole. Those U-shaped metal pins lying on the bottom of the newly purchased boat were oarlocks, she explained, which fitted onto the sides and stern of the boat, so that each of the three rowers, facing backward, could handle a pair of oars, while the fourth person, facing forward, managed the steering oar and chose the path of least resistance through the water.

Having learned that the work party was heading up the Columbia and Snake rivers into a region where gold was to be found in the sandbars, Ming recalled what Mistah Walt and his brother, Allan, had told her about the nature of the two rivers. Both were big rivers, they had said, sometimes wide, deep, and placid, sometimes narrow, rock-strewn, and filled with rapids. Frequently, strong winds blew, sometimes upriver, sometimes down. When favorable, these winds could be very useful.

"We must make sails and masts for the boats," she told Ah Fat. "We will need poles, canvas, pulleys, and ropes. I will show you how to rig them."

"Will the cost be great?"

"No. And it will save us much time and work. We will make lateen sails and rig the boats as dhows."

Checking with Chen Yu to make sure that the added expense met with his approval, Ah Fat learned that Ming Sen came from a long line of boat people, thus possessed skills that would be highly useful during their journey upriver.

"If she suggests masts and sails, by all means install them,"

Chen Yu said. "She is like a fish in water, I am told, and very wise in its ways."

Navigating the broad, tranquil reaches of the Columbia below the Cascades for the first few days, the boat crews began to acquire a measure of expertise, though Ming knew they never would become seasoned rivermen. She handled the steering oar, set the course, and supervised the trimming of sail in the lead boat; Ah Fat took charge of the second boat; while Chea Yow, who had worked for a time aboard a fishing boat before coming to America, commanded the third boat. When the wind was favorable, they hoisted sail and made a good day's run. When it was not, they rowed, making as little as eight miles a day into the strong current, head winds, and waves.

Each night, they beached the boats and camped ashore, sleeping under the open sky when the weather was good, using the sails as shelters when it rained. Rice, tea, and fish provided them with sustenance. For warmth on chill nights, they huddled together rather than build a fire, having learned from bitter experience that the less visible their camp was to travelers, the less trouble they would have with white roughs, who regarded the Chinese as fair game for molestation and thievery.

In order to pay portage charges for the boats, they worked for a week at both the Lower Cascades and The Dalles, loading and unloading freight, chopping and stacking cordwood for the riverboats, resetting ties and replacing rails in the heavily used portage railroads. Working under the direction of a white superintendent, they were not jeered at by adults or tormented by boys, for the superintendent made sure that he got full value in labor received for the money he expended in wages, thus would brook no interruption from outsiders. Of course, when they had completed their jobs and resumed traveling, they again became objects of scorn and abuse.

Though Ah Fat did not try to shelter her when she was called upon to perform physical tasks within her strength, he came quickly to her aid when brute power was needed. As headman, he did not tolerate laziness or shirking, but he was a shrewd judge of how much manpower a certain task required, and he utilized the labor in his charge to maximum effect.

Initiative and imagination were not strong points in the makeup of the Chinese laborer, Ming knew. Left to his own devices, he would do a specific task the same way time after time, no matter how awkward the manner was in which he had learned to do it. Even when shown a better way, he would not readily accept it. He must be made to repeat it over and over again, until finally he did it *this* way because *this* was the way he had done it so many times before.

Few of the clansmen could swim; none swam with Ming Sen's proficiency. They feared water; she felt at home in it. More and more as the boats moved into the barren, bleak desert country of the interior, Ah Fat came to depend on her judgment when difficult rapids were encountered.

Including the time taken to work out portage fare for the boats at the Cascades and The Dalles, it took the party three weeks to ascend the Columbia to the mouth of the Snake. Summer had come now, but with sources high in the mountains, the Snake River ran in full, tumultuous flood. Not until the party reached Lewiston, one hundred and forty miles east of the Snake's juncture with the Columbia, did the crest of the high-water period begin to fall. By then, the party had turned south toward Hell's Canyon, where Ming knew they would encounter the most dangerous rapids in the river.

For two days, the party camped on a sandbar half a mile upstream from Lewiston. Ah Fat and Chea Yow went into town, stocked up on supplies for the next six months, and talked to local Chinese merchants about the prospects for work in the area. The news they brought back to their clansmen was not good.

"Bad times have come to the inland provinces of *Gum Shan*," Ah Fat told them. "Jobs are scarce, money is tight, and white workingmen are angry. They seek someone to blame. We Chinese are hated here in Idaho, just as we are in Portland. Our friends advise us to stay away from white settlements and mining camps. We must work for ourselves, they say, in places where we can remain inconspicuous."

"Is there gold in these places?" Chea Sun asked.

"Not in great amounts. But our needs are small. If we work hard, we can pan two or three dollars a day apiece in flour gold, which is found on the sandbars. This is better than idleness."

Flour gold held little appeal for white men, Ah Fat told his clansmen, for separating the tiny flakes from the fine white sand with which they were mixed required long hours of work and a great deal of patience. Along the granite-lined streams that formed the headwaters of the Snake, white prospectors had placer-mined for years, taking fortunes in coarse gold nuggets from their arrastras, rockers, sluice boxes, and large-scale diggings. But unless a claim paid at least ten dollars a day, the white man soon deserted it and moved on in search of richer fields.

When spring snow-melt and· summer flooding turned the streams of the high country into raging torrents, a great deal of gold-bearing rock washed down into the Snake from its tributaries. As the peak of the floods passed, the river dropped deposits of float gold on sandbars in the depths of Hell's Canyon, so that each year new finds could be made by searchers not greedy for large returns. When the runoff had been extremely high, small nuggets sometimes were deposited in substantial amounts below particularly strong eddies. This was the sort of strike Ah Fat hoped to make.

Ming knew that Allan Randall lived in Lewiston and had mining interests upriver; she also knew that Mistah Walt had made plans to visit him this summer. But it did not even occur to her to inquire about them or attempt to see them. As Ah Fat's wife and a member of his party, she felt herself completely cut off from the world of the white man. By accident, she had become a part of that world for a while. But now that her circumstances had changed, she accepted her fate without complaint—and would do whatever she had to do to survive.

15

Camped on a long, curving sandbar just below the mouth of
the Golden Girl, Lord Farley Windham Smythe was enjoying
his stay in Hell's Canyon immensely. The remoteness of the
mining site, the colorful history of the area, and the rugged
yet surprisingly beautiful terrain were deeply satisfying to his
love of adventure, his appetite for excitement, and his appreciation of human drama.

Because of the steepness of the canyon wall rising from the
Oregon shore of the Snake, the mine site and the sandbar
below it lay in shadow as the late afternoon sun dropped beneath the canyon's rim. Sitting on a folding canvas stool in
front of his tent, Lord Smythe wore his usual summertime,
back-country dress: hobnailed hiking boots, calf-length tan
stockings, khaki shorts, and a light-brown, short-sleeved shirt.
For the moment, his pith helmet had been put aside.

Though his legs and arms had acquired a healthy tan, his
face remained ruddy and his nose bright red—a peculiarity of
skin pigmentation that he long ago had gotten used to, just as
he had accepted the fact that while his hair remained auburn,
his stiff, neatly clipped mustache had turned pure white.

Higher up the slope, workmen were moving in and out of
the mine, clearing rock from the last blast of the day. When
they had finished, he and the Welsh mining superintendent,
Barney Breen, would go into the tunnel, inspect it, and plan
the next day's work. While he waited, he passed the time by
writing a letter to his sixteen-year-old niece, Elizabeth Olivia
Smythe, who took a great interest in the history of the American West:

No doubt you have heard of Chief Joseph, one of the greatest Indian leaders his race has ever known. This was the heart of his homeland. When directed by the United States Government to leave the Wallowa Valley in Oregon and take his people to the Nez Perce reservation in Idaho, he asked for three months to make the move. He was given only thirty days. Laden with all his tribe's lodges, possessions, old men, women, and children, with six thousand of their cattle and horses, Chief Joseph led his people down from the high mountain valley which had been their summer home to a point on the Snake River only a little way upstream from the spot on which I now am encamped.

Curiously enough, the trail taken by the Indians from the Wallowa Valley in Oregon to the Indian reservation and white settlements in Idaho now is used by an unscrupulous band of men euphemistically called "cowboys." Actually they are thieves whose only means of livelihood is rounding up cattle and horses left behind by the Nez Perces or stealing them from white ranchers who have moved into the Wallowa Valley, driving them to Idaho, and selling them to buyers who ask no questions as to how the animals were acquired.

Because of our remoteness from the market place, we are forced to buy beef on the hoof from them for our mess hall, though you may rest assured we watch them very closely when they come into camp, for they are not to be trusted. . . .

A disturbance that had begun some moments ago now grew to such a degree that Lord Smythe could no longer ignore it. Closing his writing pad, he put it in his tent, donned his pith helmet, and walked toward the group of men who were arguing with one another a hundred feet away.

"I say, old chaps, what's the row all about?"

"Frank Vane, 'ere, wants to open a grog shop on our property," Barney Breen said angrily. "I told 'im if 'e tries, I'll bloody well bust 'is nose and kick 'is arse into the river."

"It's a free country," Frank Vane said sullenly. "Far as nose-bustin' and ass-kickin' is concerned, any goddam Limey tries it on me is gonna get his goddam head shot off."

Red-faced, chunky, and well muscled, Barney Breen, the Welsh mining superintendent, long since had demonstrated his ability to discipline workmen with his sharp tongue, nimble foot, and rock-hard fists. But the four men he was confronting now were not workmen; they were members of the band of "cowboys" about which Lord Smythe had just written his niece. All carried rifles on their saddles and wore holstered revolvers. Frank Vane, leader of the group, was dismounted. The other three men, whom Lord Smythe knew as Matt Le-Croix, Tom Crowell, and Zeke Hewitt, remained seated on their horses, gazing down at him and the mining superintendent with a contempt they made no effort to conceal. Behind them, a string of laden pack horses grazed on scattered tufts of bunch grass.

Every two or three weeks when driving horses and cattle to Idaho, Frank Vane and his cohorts stopped at the mining camp, sold a few steers to the mess hall, and took orders for whatever supplies the cook wished them to bring back from the Idaho settlements. Workmen would order tobacco and personal needs, which Vane later would deliver and sell for a modest profit. Since alcohol in any form was forbidden on mine property, it had not been a problem until now.

"Your pack horses are carrying strong spirits, I take it?" Lord Smythe said pleasantly.

"You take it right, Buster," Vane answered.

"My name is Farley, Mister Vane. Farley Smythe. The company I represent has made a substantial investment in this venture—"

"You don't say!" Vane sneered. Glancing down at Lord Smythe's bare knees, he laughed. "Then how come they send a man wearin' little-boy pants to run it for them?"

In Lord Smythe's opinion, ridiculing a person's mode of

dress was the height of boorishness, but he chose to ignore Vane's bad manners. A tall, rugged-looking man in his early thirties, Frank Vane had long yellow hair, a droopy mustache, and washed-out blue eyes. He was rumored to have killed several men, which did not unduly impress Lord Smythe. It took little courage to kill.

"Really, Mister Vane—"

"My name is Frank."

"Really, Frank, I have no wish to be unfriendly. It is just that experience has taught me that alcohol and mining do not mix. Therefore, if your intention is to set up a grog shop—"

"A saloon, Farley. A plain and simple tent saloon, where a workingman can wet his whistle after hours and on his day off. What's wrong with that?"

"Our workmen don't 'ave a day off," Breen grunted testily. "They work an honest ten-hour day, seven days a week, for good wages, with room and board furnished free. But on or off the job, they're not allowed to drink in camp."

Above at the mouth of the tunnel, the last of the ore cars had been hauled out and dumped. It was now six o'clock; the long workday was done. Mules were being unhitched and led down the slope to be watered and fed; tired, dirt-grimed workmen were moving toward the mess hall, a washup, supper, and a long evening of nowhere to go and nothing to do. Overhearing the argument, they paused and muttered among themselves.

"What's the squabble?"

"He wants to open a saloon."

"Here?"

"That's what he says."

"That's a great idea!"

"Hey, fellas," one of the workmen called out, "you got any beer in them packs?"

"Sure have," Matt LeCroix said with a grin. "Ten barrels of the best Dutch beer ever brewed in Idaho."

"Got any Bourbon?" another miner yelled.

"Eight cases," Tom Crowell answered. "Distilled by a man who learned his trade in Kentucky."

"To hell with beer and Bourbon!" another workman shouted. "You got any Snake River moonshine?"

"You betcha!" Zeke Hewitt replied with a laugh. "Twenty jugs of it."

"Where's this saloon gonna be?"

"Who cares *where?* Just tell us when you'll open for business!"

An enthusiastic cheer went up from the crowd, which now included most of the crew. *This could get sticky,* Lord Smythe mused. The men had been working hard and had not had a drink for several weeks. Far be it from him to begrudge a thirsty workman a pint or two of beer or a few shot glasses of whisky after a long day underground. But if a saloon was to be opened near the mine, it would have to be strictly regulated as to when and what it served its customers .

Frank Vane looked questioningly at Lord Smythe. "Well, Farley, what do you say? Any objection if we pitch our tent on the upper end of the sandbar?"

Noting that Barney Breen's face had turned several shades redder than usual, Lord Smythe laid a cautioning hand on his arm. In this sort of situation, physical violence should be resorted to only after all other means of persuasion had failed.

"Under certain conditions, I would not object to a saloon being operated in this vicinity," Lord Smythe said calmly. "However, it would have to observe strict rules—"

"Which would be?"

"It would be open for only one hour—six to seven—between the end of the workday and the serving of the evening meal. Its proprietor could sell any alcoholic drink he wished during this period. During the supper hour—seven to eight P.M.—the establishment would close. After supper, it would be permitted to open again for two hours—that is, from eight to ten P.M. During this period, nothing but beer would be served."

"Hey, that sounds fair enough to me!" one of the workmen cried. "Don't it to you, Kevin?"

"Sure, it suits me fine. Who wants to drill rock with a hang-over?"

"I'll save my big sprees for Lewiston," another workman said, with a nod of approval. "But a couple of beers after work would taste great."

Frank Vane hesitated, then turned to his companions and grunted, "What do you think, boys?"

"With only three hours a day to stay open, it'll take us weeks to sell our stock," Matt LeCroix objected. "We got better ways to spend our time than running a saloon."

"This ain't the only sandbar on the river," Tom Crowell muttered. "Why can't we pitch our tent just around the bend upstream?"

"Hell, yes!" Zeke Hewitt exclaimed. "This prissy-lookin' Britisher don't own the whole river. Let's pitch our tent around the bend and stay open as long as we please. If he don't like it, he can lump it."

Frank Vane looked challengingly at Lord Smythe. "What do you say to that?"

Under his restraining hand, Lord Smythe felt the muscles of Barney Breen's forearm stiffen. "Lemme bust 'is bloody nose!" Breen pleaded. "Lemme work the blighter over!"

"If you attack him, he'll use his gun," Lord Smythe said quietly. "There's a better way to handle this. "

"Speak up!" Vane jeered. "What will you do if we tell you to go to the devil? Just what in the hell will you do?"

Lord Smythe took off his pith helmet and handed it to Barney Breen. As he unbuttoned his shirt, he said softly, "What will I do? Why, sir, much as I deplore violence, I shall be forced to give you a sound thrashing. Be a good lad, Barney—have the ring set up and the boxing gloves brought down from the mess hall. I'm sure Mister Vane will have no objection to fighting under Marquis of Queensberry rules."

16

The four would-be saloon proprietors stared at Lord Smythe in surprised silence. So did Barney Breen and the mine workmen. Though in good physical condition for a man his age, which was forty-five, Lord Smythe was six inches shorter, twenty pounds lighter, and fifteen years older than Frank Vane. In a rough-and-tumble fight, he would stand no chance at all. But that was not the kind of fight Lord Smythe had proposed.

"If ever I heard a dare from a real sport, that's one!" shouted Paddy Ryan, foreman of the rock-drilling crew. "Will you take it, Frank Vane? Will you step into the ring with Farley Smythe?"

"'Ring'?" Vane muttered, scowling. "What ring?"

"The boxing ring we'll be makin' in two shakes of a lamb's tail, if you accept his challenge."

"Boxin' ain't my style," Vane said uncomfortably.

"Haven't you ever seen a prizefight?"

"Sure. But I've never been in one."

"Thirty-six bouts I've fought myself, in mining camps from Butte to Bisbee," Paddy Ryan said proudly. "Never a one did I lose till my legs and wind went bad. 'Tis a grand sport, boxing. But you haven't answered my question, Vane. Will you put on the gloves and step into the ring with Farley Smythe?"

"Well, I ain't afraid of him—"

"Good! I'll referee the bout. Choose your second. Strip to the waist, take off your boots, and loosen up with a few knee-bends. After a day a-horseback, you're bound to be stiff in the joints—"

"Now wait a minute, goddam it!"

But no one was listening or waiting. As Lord Smythe had anticipated, the prospect of the highest form of entertainment a mining camp could offer excited everyone to such a degree that the match could be stopped only by the man challenged cravenly backing down, which he doubted Vane would do. Frank Vane's companions were especially excited.

"Hot damn—this'll be fun!" Zeke Hewitt exclaimed.

"Gimme your gunbelt, Frank," Matt LeCroix said. "I'll take care of it for you."

"Lemme help you off with your boots," Tom Crowell said. "They're no good when you're prizefightin' in a sandy ring."

"Take off your shirt and hat," Zeke Hewitt said. "I'll be your second."

"What do I need a second for?"

"A prizefighter has to have a second. That's Marquis of Queensberry rules."

"But I ain't no prizefighter! I don't know a goddam thing about prizefightin'!"

"That don't matter, Frank. I'm an expert. With me in your corner tellin' you what to do, we won't have a bit of trouble whippin' this fancy-pants Britisher. We're younger and stronger than he is. We'll wear him down. We'll keep chargin' and swingin'—"

Under Barney Breen's supervision, a square ring sixteen feet on a side was marked out on a level, reasonably firm section of sandbar. Posts were set at each corner, ropes were stretched and tied, and canvas stools were brought for the two fighters, their seconds, and the timekeeper. Paddy Ryan insisted that the spectators be distributed evenly around the four sides of the ring so that all would have an equally good chance to see.

Chang, the moon-faced young Chinese cook's helper whom Barney had sent up to the mess hall to fetch the boxing gloves, returned with them, gave them to the mine superintendent, and asked excitedly, "Mistah boss-man gonna fight cowboy?"

"Right."

"You gonna bet on Mistah boss-man?"

"Sure."

"Then I gonna bet on Mistah boss-man, too."

Joining the other Chinese laborers, Chang, who was an avid prizefight fan, chattered with them in singsong Cantonese, telling them what was about to happen. The white workmen were eagerly laying wagers among themselves and with Frank Vane's companions on how many rounds the bout would last and who its winner would be. Giving one pair of gloves to Paddy Ryan, who took them to Vane's corner, Barney Breen brought the other pair to Lord Smythe.

"Can I be your second, sir?"

"Certainly."

" 'E's a bad 'un, sir," Breen muttered, as he helped Lord Smythe into the gloves. "You should 'ave let me fight 'im."

"Matter of protocol, old boy. He asked me what I would do."

"What you should do, sir, is tell me to boot 'is arse into the river. Then 'e'd 'ave to fight me or show the white feather."

"Our workmen wouldn't blame him for not fighting you, Barney. But if he refused to fight me, they would laugh him out of camp."

" 'E's got reach, 'eight, and weight on you, sir. Don't let 'im bull you over. Go for 'is peepers. If 'e can't see you, 'e can't 'it you."

"Thank you, Barney. That's excellent advice."

In the opposite corner, Frank Vane stared distastefully down at the gloves that Zeke Hewitt was lacing around his wrists. They had very little padding in them, thus would take little force out of a blow so far as its recipient was concerned. But they would give some protection to the hands of the fighter wearing them.

"We've got to watch his quick darters, which he'll keep pokin' in your face," Zeke Hewitt said. "When we see our chance, we'll duck under them, give him a left lifter on the chin, then a right hooker to his jaw—"

"Where do you get this 'we' stuff?" Vane grunted. "You gonna be in the ring with me?"

"It's just a prizefight way of speakin', Frank. Do what I tell you and we'll take him."

Referee Paddy Ryan called the two contestants and their seconds to the center of the ring. "We'll fight mining camp Marquis of Queensberry rules," he said. "No biting, gouging, or head butting. No hitting below the belt nor when a man is down. When a contestant goes to one knee, the round is over. Both fighters must retire to their corners—"

"For how long?" Vane asked.

"One minute. The timekeeper will give you a ten-second warning. He'll sing out: 'Come to time!' Then you must return to the center of the ring and resume fighting—"

"Sounds like a waste of time to me," Vane grumbled. "Why can't we just slug away at each other till one of us goes down and stays down?"

"Because boxing is fought by sporting rules," Paddy Ryan said sharply. "You'll abide by them, Frank Vane, or you'll take off those gloves and get out of camp."

"I was just tryin' to keep it simple."

"If it's a roughhouse brawl you want, I'll oblige," Barney Breen said pugnaciously. "In or out of the ring, wi' no referee or rules."

"Hey, we're puttin' on a first-class fight!" Zeke Hewitt exclaimed. "Don't go messin' it up, you dumb British bastard!"

Taking two quick steps forward, Barney Breen seized Hewitt by the shirtfront with his left hand, balled his right hand into a fist, and shook it under the man's nose.

"I'm Welsh, not British, and I know who my father was, you stupid Yankee son of a bitch!"

"Don't you bad-mouth my mother!" Hewitt bristled. "She was a good woman!"

"So was my father! A good man, I mean. Now is Vane going to fight Farley Smythe by fair and square boxing rules or fight me wi' no rules at all? Tell 'im to make up 'is bloody mind. Or maybe *you'd* like to fight me?"

"I say, gentlemen, let's not lose our tempers," Lord Smythe said soothingly, moving forward to pull Breen away from Hewitt while Paddy Ryan pulled Hewitt away from Breen. "Frank will abide by the rules, I dare say. Won't you, Frank?"

"Sure—if you'll tell me what they are."

"That's my job as referee," Paddy Ryan said. "Do you have any questions?"

"A couple. How long is a round?"

"That depends."

"On what?"

"On how long it takes a contestant to slip, fall, or be knocked to one knee. In the best prizefight I ever saw, the shortest round lasted eighteen seconds, the longest two and a half minutes."

"How many rounds did it go?"

"Eighty-four."

"*Eighty-four!*" Vane exclaimed. "How long did it last, for Christ's sake?"

"Two hours and five seconds."

Zeke Hewitt, who had been listening with growing interest, shook his head in amazement. "That must have been one hell of a prizefight. Who were the bruisers?"

"James Dwyer and Patsy Foy."

"Where did they fight?"

"In Silver City, down in the southwestern part of Idaho. Though it happened twenty years ago, I can still remember every blow. . . ."

"*Two hours and five seconds?*" Vane muttered. "How could they fight that long?"

"Superb physical condition," Paddy Ryan said, obviously pleased to display his knowledge of the sport. "The lads trained six weeks for the match."

"Well, this fight ain't gonna last more'n five minutes," Vane said, scowling at Lord Smythe. "You ready, Farley?"

"If you are, old boy."

"Go to your corners," Paddy Ryan said. "Chang, you set to keep time?"

"You betcha! Got bell. Got watchee."

"Give 'em the ten-second warning, then call 'em to time."

Holding a school bell poised in his right hand, peering down at the gold-plated watch in his left hand, Chang squealed, "Tlen-slecond warning!"

"Go git him, Frank!" Matt LeCroix yelled.

"Show him your stuff, Farley!" a workman cried.

Gazing across the ring, Lord Smythe felt the warm sand soft and grainy under his bare feet, a reminder that fancy footwork would be of little use. On the other hand, it would cushion a fall far better than a hard-surfaced ring. From the impatient way Frank Vane was staring at him, Lord Smythe guessed that he would waste no time in sparring but would attempt to end the fight as quickly as possible.

"Keep 'im off balance," Barney Breen muttered. "Go for 'is peepers."

Ringing the bell, Chang cried: "Clum to tlime!"

Instead of rushing across the ring, Frank Vane moved cautiously out of his corner, holding his elbows and clenched fists together in front of his chest and face, peering over his knuckles with suspicious eyes as he waited to see what his opponent was going to do. Lord Smythe moved to the center of the ring. With his left fist held at chest height and his right fist poised in front of his chin, he waited for Vane to make his move.

Staying well out of reach, Vane shuffled to his right in heavy, flat-footed fashion until he had made a half circuit of the ring, stopped, stood still for several seconds, then shuffled back to his left until he reached the spot from which he had begun. Though a full minute had passed, neither man had struck a blow.

"Give us some action!" a workman cried.

"Now, Frank!" Zeke Hewitt yelled.

Vane charged like an enraged bear, swinging a wild left and a roundhouse right, either one of which would have ended the match, if it had connected. But neither blow landed, for Lord Smythe pulled back his head, sidestepped, and then gave Vane two stinging lefts and a stiff right to the face. Backing away, Vane stared at him in surprise.

"Quick, ain't you?"

"Not really. You gave me an opening."

"Well, see what you can do this time!" Vane grunted, and charged again.

Lord Smythe managed to evade a flurry of haymaker swings, in turn landing two capital lefts to his adversary's face. But as he attempted to follow up with a right, Vane ducked his head, bulled in, and caught the older man with a jolting right to the solar plexus. The wind whistled out of Lord Smythe's lungs. Gasping for breath, he went rubber-kneed, sagged, and dropped to the ground. As he fell, Vane grabbed him by the shoulder with his left hand and drew his right hand back to strike.

Shouting angrily, Barney Breen scrambled through the ropes and charged into the ring from one side; with an indignant yell, Zeke Hewitt climbed through the ropes and bolted into the ring from the other side. Paddy Ryan stepped between the two contestants.

"End of round!" the referee shouted, seizing Vane by the elbows. "Go to your corner!"

"Foul!" Breen cried. "'E tried to 'it Farley when 'e was down!"

"He did no such of a thing!" Hewitt yelled. "Farley fell down on purpose, tryin' to draw a foul!"

"End of lound!" Chang sang out as he furiously shook the school bell. "Flighters will go to clorners!"

"Lemme go!" Vane muttered, struggling to break free of Paddy's grasp. "I'll finish him off!"

"You touch 'im, I'll finish *you* off!" Breen cried, lunging for Vane.

"Stay away from my man, damn you!" Hewitt yelled, lunging for Breen.

With the two fighters, their seconds, and the referee scuffling inside the ring and thirty excited spectators shoving, shouting, and arguing with one another outside the ring, the prizefight seemed on the verge of degenerating into a free-for-all. But Paddy Ryan, an old hand at managing such affairs, took firm control.

"Fighters to your corners! Seconds out of the ring!"

Reluctantly, they obeyed his orders. Crossing to Vane's corner, he shook an admonishing finger at him. "Two points I'm chargin' against you, Frank Vane, for layin' hands on a man when he was down." He turned toward Lord Smythe's corner. "One point I'm chargin' against you, Barney Breen, for comin' into the ring without permission."

"Ha!" Zeke Hewitt snorted. "Serves him right!"

"And one point against you, Zeke Hewitt," Paddy snapped, turning back, "for doin' likewise. Now mind the rules, all of you, else I'll be stoppin' the fight and declarin' him winner who has the least points charged against his side."

"Bully for you, Paddy!" a spectator shouted. "Keep 'em up to snuff!"

"That's the ticket!" another man cried. "Make 'em fight fair and square!"

Sitting on the stool in his corner, Lord Smythe was having trouble breathing. Barney Breen mopped his face with a damp towel.

"Did 'e 'urt you bad, sir?"

"Knocked the wind out of me. But it's coming back."

"Stay away from him for a few rounds. Keep workin' on 'is peepers."

"Righto."

During the next few rounds, Lord Smythe fought cautiously, sidestepping, backing away, keeping his left hand in Vane's face, throwing his right hand only when Vane was off balance and unable to counter. Both the second and third rounds ended with Vane going down, not from Lord Smythe's blows but from his own clumsiness, the younger man tripping over his own feet after missed swings.

Two minutes into the fifth round, Lord Smythe caught a looping right to his left temple that made his head ring. As he backed away, Vane charged, missed with wildly swung lefts and rights, locked his arms around Lord Smythe's neck in a bear hug, tripped him, and bore him to the ground. By accident or design, Vane's right knee came up into Lord Smythe's groin with painful force.

"'E done it on purpose," Barney Breen said indignantly as he toweled his employer's face and chest dry. "Shall we claim a foul?"

"No way to prove it," Lord Smythe said, shaking his head. "Purely a waste of time." He peered across the ring. "I do believe his left eye is swollen shut."

Breen nodded. "So 'tis. Go to work on the right 'un."

For the next four rounds, Lord Smythe did that, continually circling to Vane's blind side while he peppered away at the good eye. Even with his vision cut in half, Vane was landing punishing blows more often, for Lord Smythe was beginning to tire. Having learned the trick of clenching, tripping his opponent, and then falling on him to end a round, Vane used it to bring the sixth, seventh, and eighth rounds to a close, though in the ninth Lord Smythe managed to reverse the trick, tripping Vane and then falling on him so heavily that he gave a pained grunt of surprise.

"'Ow you 'oldin' up?" Barney Breen asked solicitously as Lord Smythe leaned back with his eyes closed and his chest heaving.

"Let's face it, Barney. I'm not the man I used to be."

"'Oo is?"

"But I have one more good round left in me, I dare say. I shall attempt to end it in the tenth."

"Don't strain yourself, sir. You've put up a good fight."

"One more round, Barney. With a bit of luck, I can take him. There's a trick I learned in the Orient that may surprise him—"

"Is it legal?"

"Perfectly legal, Barney. Startling, perhaps. But legal. You see, oriental fighters go into a kind of a trance, focusing all their mental, nervous, and muscular energy into a single moment of concentrated, explosive power—"

"Tlen-slecond warning!" Chang cried out.

"They do what?" Barney asked as the crowd began to roar.

Lord Smythe did not hear or answer. Closing his eyes, he willed himself to think only of the final effort he would make, the final blow he would strike. If effort and blow failed, he would be finished, of course, for the secret of the trick was to hold nothing in reserve.

"Clum to tlime!"

From the opposite corner, Frank Vane moved out to the center of the ring, fists held at the ready, left eye swollen shut, but still strong and confident. Like a man in a trance, Lord Smythe stood up and walked out to meet him. Instead of holding his gloves up in his usual boxing style, his hands drooped laxly at his side and he appeared utterly defenseless as he moved toward Vane. As he came within reach, Vane scowled at him.

"What the hell is the matter with you?"

Tensing his body with sudden effort, Lord Smythe let out an inhuman, blood-curdling yell. Because it was totally unexpected, Frank Vane dropped his guard for a moment. Putting everything he had into the blow, Lord Smythe swung a crushing right against the left side of Vane's face, landing it flush on the hinge of the jawbone.

Falling face forward like a sledged ox, Frank Vane pitched soundlessly to the sand.

A stunned silence lay over the ring and the spectators for several seconds. Then bedlam broke loose.

"Farley done it!" a workman cried. "He cold-cocked him!"

"Foul!" Zeke Hewitt cried. "That was a foul!"

"End of round!" Paddy shouted. "Fighters to your corners!"

Rubber-kneed and barely able to walk, Lord Smythe staggered back to his stool, sat down, and passed out. Climbing into the ring and seizing Vane by the shoulders, Zeke Hewitt dragged him toward his corner, yelling, "Foul! We claim this here fight on a foul!"

"What foul?" Referee Ryan grunted. "I didn't see no foul."

"You heard it, didn't you?"

"How can you *hear* a foul?"

"He yelled! Damn it, he yelled!"

"Nothin' wrong with that."

"It ain't in the Marquis of Queensberry rules. I know 'em by heart. There ain't one goddam word in the rules says a prizefighter can yell at his opponent like that."

"Well, there ain't no rule says he can't."

"It's a foul, I claim—"

"Disallowed! Chang, are you keepin' time?"

"You betcha! Fifteen sleconds now. Flourteen, flirteen, flelve, 'leben. Tlen-slecond warning! Tlen-slecond warning!"

"Can you make it, sir?" Barney Breen inquired solicitously. "Or do you want me to throw in the towel?"

Regaining a measure of consciousness, Lord Smythe opened his eyes and gave his second a wan smile. "I feel fine. How does *he* look?"

"'E can't find the ground with both 'ands. All you got to do is get up and walk to the middle of the ring."

"Nothing to it, old boy," Lord Smythe muttered. "Just set me on my feet and point me in the proper direction."

"Clum to tlime!" Chang squealed. "Flighters will clum to tlime!"

As he felt strong hands under his armpits lifting him to an erect stance, Lord Smythe was dimly aware that on the opposite side of the ring Frank Vane's second was assisting his opponent to his feet. Very slowly, very cautiously, Lord Smythe took a step forward. So did Frank Vane—only to fall flat on his face and lie unmoving. Lord Smythe took a second step, then a third, and stopped. Vaguely he was aware that Paddy Ryan had moved to his side, seized his right wrist, and was raising his arm high.

"I declare the winner of this prizefight to be—Farley Smythe!"

While the crowd cheered wildly, Lord Smythe responded with a feebly waved gesture of appreciation, turned back toward his corner, took two steps, and collapsed in Barney Breen's arms.

"Not the man I used to be, Barney. But I gave it the best I had."

"You taught 'im a lesson 'e ain't likely to forget, sir! The cheek of 'im, thinkin' 'e could set up a grog shop near *our* camp!"

"Let's be charitable, Barney. Tell Zeke Hewitt we'll buy his stock of spirits at a fair price and part friends, if he so desires. We'll run our own pub under the rules I offered them. Put Chang in charge. Now if I may impose upon your good nature and strong arm to help me to my tent, I should like to lie down for a while. I'm feeling a bit under the weather."

17

As the bow of the *Annie Faxon* gently bumped the Lewiston dock, Allan Randall, standing beside Walt at the starboard rail of the big cargo boat, gestured affectionately at the small, narrow stern-wheeler moored in the next berth upstream.

"There's the *Hell's Angel.* Ain't she a beauty?"

"She looks like a toy, compared to the boats we've been on."

"She's undersize, all right, but she's no toy," Allan said with a smile. "A big boat is useless in Hell's Canyon. In places, the river narrows down to sixty feet, with turns so sharp a boat has to spin on a dime and give five cents change. As the river goes down, which it does each summer, a boat drawing more than two feet can't go above Wild Goose Rapid."

"What does the *Angel* draw?"

"Nine inches light; eighteen inches fully loaded. She can carry a hundred tons."

"Did you design her yourself?"

"Oh, I stole a bit here, cribbed a bit there, and improvised on the design of boats I've worked on or seen. Actually, her dimensions are those of a boat I saw and liked several years ago on a lake up in British Columbia, the *Lady Dufferin.* She was a side-wheeler and didn't get nearly as much horsepower per pound of engine and boiler as I knew I could get with a specially designed power plant. I changed her into a stern-wheeler, put extra cross-bracing in her bow, mounted a steam-powered capstan forward, and moved her pilothouse aft a few feet for better balance."

"You use the capstan for climbing rapids?"

Allan nodded. "Give me a few thousand feet of steel wire cable and a deadman to hook onto, I can put the *Angel* up a tree. You'll see when we go upriver next week."

As they crossed the gangplank to the dock, a voice from the pilothouse above hailed them sharply. "Allan, you rascal! Don't you forget what I told you!"

"Never fear," Allan answered, giving the master of the *Annie Faxon* a salute as he turned and looked up. "I always keep my word, Captain Gray."

"Well, you'll keep *my* words—or I'll know the reason why."

"You bet."

Walking up the slanting, unsteady wooden dock, Walt was having trouble maintaining his balance. Allan put a hand under his elbow and steadied him. As they reached firmer footing on the waterfront street above, Walt gave his brother a searching look.

"What words is he talking about?"

"The ones he wrote on the check, I suppose."

"How many shares of the Golden Girl did you sell him?"

"Two hundred. But he made the check payable to me only when accompanied by a receipt of delivery of the shares to him." Allan sighed. "The gall of the old boy! Can you imagine anybody not trusting me?"

"I can," Walt murmured grimly. "Even if he were your own brother. . . ."

Three days of sorting through the piles of reports, forms, unanswered letters, and undone paperwork that had accumulated in every corner of Allan Randall's office convinced Walt that the *Snake River Mining & Transportation Company* either needed to employ an arsonist, who would solve the company's problems with kerosene and match, or hire competent legal and clerical help to bring order out of chaos.

Other than filing mineral claims and writing down the names of the people to whom he had sold stock, Allan had done no paperwork at all.

"Mrs. Shelby told me she would handle it," Allan said

vaguely. "But one of her relatives took sick. Her sister, I think it was, in Seattle. Or Butte. Or maybe it was Boise. Anyway, she asked for a week off and traveling money. So of course I gave it to her."

"How long ago was this?"

"About a month. Maybe six weeks."

"You haven't heard from her since?"

"Not directly. You see, she was a widow and she didn't have any family here. She got lonesome, I guess. She'd been a schoolteacher, she said, and claimed to be a real whiz at book-keeping, though actually what I hired her for was to come in a couple of afternoons a week and tidy up the place. When I started selling stock, she began to give me a hand with the mail, sorting out checks and cash, sending out certificates, making deposits at the bank—"

"And she went to Seattle or Butte or Boise six weeks ago to visit a sick sister and hasn't been heard from since. Exit Mrs. Shelby. With an undetermined amount of cash."

Allan grinned sheepishly. "My trouble is I trust people too much. I've got no head for paperwork, Walt. Can you straighten out this mess for me?"

"I can try. But you've got to give me a free hand."

"You've got it."

As a first step, Walt hired a manager and a bookkeeper to put the company's office files in order and retained a local attorney to help him with the legal work. Since this should have been done six months ago, he told Allan, it was going to be a long, arduous chore putting the company into a tenable position from which it could defend itself against charges of fraud brought by disgruntled stockholders—

"But they're not disgruntled, Walt!" Allan objected. "They're happy as clams! They think the Golden Girl is the biggest bonanza ever discovered!"

"How much gold has it produced?"

"We're just beginning operations. We've got to finish the tunnel, set up the stamp mill, get out the ore, crush it, smelt it—"

"All of which is exciting as hell for you and the stock-holders—but costs a hell of a lot of money."

"We'll get it back ten times over."

"Maybe. Maybe not. But whatever happens, you'd better be prepared to prove that you had a legitimate prospect, raised money to work it by selling stock in a legitimate way, and can account for every dollar you spent. Otherwise, if the mine goes sour, your happy-as-clams stockholders will string you up by the thumbs. When do I get a look at the Golden Girl?"

"Tomorrow," Allan said cheerfully. "We'll head upriver at daylight."

The crew of the *Hell's Angel*, Walt learned when he boarded the boat early the next morning, consisted of an engineer, two firemen who doubled as deckhands, and its owner-pilot-captain. Never had he seen Allan in such high spirits. Carrying a carpetbag containing a change of clothes, a quart of whisky, and ten thousand dollars in paper money with which to meet the month's payroll and camp expenses, he helped Walt cross the gangplank and then paused on deck to introduce him to the crew.

"Walt, meet my chief engineer, Scotty Douglas, my first mate, Pete Norberg, and my second mate, Joe Warren. Gentlemen, this is my lawyer brother, who's going to make me toe the line from now on."

"Who's going to try, you mean," Walt said, shaking hands. "Glad to meet you, gentlemen."

"As you shall observe, I run a very high-class boat," Allan said. "All officers, no crew. Mister Warren, are the fuel bunkers full?"

"Aye, sir. Plumb full."

"Mister Douglas, is steam pressure up?"

"Aye, sir. One hundred eighty-two pounds."

"Very good! Mister Norberg, prepare to cast off your lines." Allan started to climb the steps to the pilothouse, then paused with a frown. "Now if somebody will please tell me which direction is upriver, we'll get under way."

Chuckling as if they had heard this joke many times, the engineer went below, the first mate went forward, and the second mate went aft. In the cramped confines of the pilothouse, Allan tossed the carpetbag into a corner, shoved a long-legged stool toward Walt, and motioned for him to sit down. Cocking his cap over his left eye to block out the glare of the just-risen sun, he rang for power. The stern-wheel started turning, lines were cast off, and the *Angel* moved out into the stream.

Because of the smallness of the boat, Walt felt the strength and menace of the river far more acutely than he had when aboard the *Annie Faxon*. As the boat's speed increased, he marveled that so light a craft could move so swiftly against the force of the current. Allan grinned at him.

"Lot of water coming down the Snake, this time of year. Brown as coffee with silt. But it'll start falling and clearing up in a few days."

"Are the rapids more dangerous in high water?"

"Not really. But whatever the river stage, I treat them all with respect. In flood stage, the river can bounce a ten-ton boulder along like a cork, dropping it God-knows-where. When the water goes down, if you make one mistake coming downstream at high speed, you're done for."

"Have you ever hit a rock?"

"Oh, I've kissed a few," Allan said wryly. "But gently—ever so gently. You see, a new rock in a rapid shows signs that it's there just like a new girl in town shows signs that she's a virgin. When you see those signs, you approach the rock just as you'd approach the girl. Gingerly—very gingerly."

With the morning half gone, the bluffs on either side of the Snake had closed in and grown higher. As the *Hell's Angel* churned past a tall limestone cliff looming above the right-hand shore, Allan inclined his head toward a stretch of tossing white water a few hundred yards upstream.

"Wild Goose Rapid. A bad one any time of year."

As the *Angel* neared the foot of the rapid, Walt could see that here the river was divided into two channels by an elongated island about an acre in extent. At the head of the island, a rock slide had deposited a number of immense boulders, against which the full force of the Snake pounded as it emerged from the narrow canyon upstream. It appeared to Walt that the major portion of the water and the heavier current ran in the channel to the right of the island—that is, to his right as he faced upstream.

"The water drops a good ten feet in a hundred-and-fifty-foot stretch of rapid," Allan said, slowing the boat so that it was barely making headway and easing it toward a slack-water pool at the foot of Wild Goose. "What you've got to watch out for is where the water coming downriver hits the rock wall to the right, then is forced out and back so hard that part of the rapid is running as fast upstream as the rest of it is running downstream. If you cross the dividing line under full power, your boat will spin around, get caught broadside, and be swept under. Wild Goose can be a killer."

"If the right-hand channel is so bad," Walt asked, "why don't you take the left-hand channel? It looks easier."

"Sometimes I do," Allan said, nodding. "But not today. I want to show you a little trick I invented."

By now, the bow of the *Angel* had been eased toward an object that was floating and bobbing in the water. As it drew abeam, Pete Norberg leaned over the rail, caught it with a boat hook, and pulled it aboard. The object was a small metal barrel, Walt saw, empty and sealed to be watertight. Attached to it was a stout, flexible, steel-wire cable. As Walt watched, the first mate unfastened the cable from the barrel, secured the loop on the cable's end to a metal dog on the steam-powered capstan, and waggled his left hand in a signal to take up the slack.

"We set a deadman fifteen hundred feet upstream on the right-hand bank," Allan said, raising his voice so that it could be heard over the thunder of the rapids. "With the capstan

pulling and the stern wheel pushing, we'll climb Wild Goose
with no trouble at all."

"What if the deadman gives way?"

"Don't worry about that. It's anchored in solid rock."

"Do you use this sort of setup at other rapids?"

"Only at the three worst ones," Allan answered. "Wild
Goose, Mountain Sheep, and Imnaha. And then only at certain stages of water. Truth is, with a couple of rock drillers
and a good powder monkey, I could blast out all the rocks
and reefs that give the *Angel* trouble on the upper Snake. But
it would take several weeks and cost a lot of money."

Reaching slack water above Wild Goose Rapid, Allan
slowed the *Hell's Angel* so that the boat barely maintained
headway against the current of the river, reversed power on
the capstan, slacked off the cable, and let it sink into the
water. When the end secured to the capstan was reached,
Pete Norberg lifted the loop off the metal dog, attached the
metal barrel to it, and then tossed the barrel over the side.
Watching it float downstream, Walt shook his head in admira-
tion.

"That's a clever trick, all right. What do you do when you
come downriver—reverse the process?"

"At first, I did. But as soon as I'd learned the rapid, I just
pointed the boat into it and charged full speed ahead. The
Angel knows her way home."

18

As the party of Chinese laborers moved up the Snake River, the lava bluffs rising in convoluted folds from either shore grew higher, the canyon through which the river flowed grew deeper, and the rapids became more violent. Sails were of little use here, for following winds were rare. Time and again the boats had to be unloaded, their contents carried around rapids over slick, treacherous pathways through the rocks, then the empty boats lined upstream by the combined brute strength of all the members of the work party.

During the week it took the party to reach its destination, the only steamboat to navigate these waters, the *Hell's Angel*, was occasionally seen by the Chinese. This was Allan Randall's boat, Ming knew. As the small stern-wheeler churned past one afternoon, she saw him leaning out of the pilothouse window as he steered, his cap jauntily perched on the side of his head, a friendly smile on his face as he shouted a greeting and lifted a hand in casual salute.

Sure that he did not recognize her, she waved back, as did the other Chinese. But her heart thumped wildly as she remembered the week Allan Randall had spent in his brother's apartment during the period when Mistah Walt lay unconscious, lingering between life and death.

When Allan first appeared, he had been hearty, voluble, and determined to bully the doctors into *making* his brother get well. Ming had readily deferred to his demands regarding treatment and care, thinking that he and the three white doctors he had brought in to consult on the case were the best judges of what must be done. She stayed at the bedside as a nurse, doing whatever the doctors told her to do. But when the chest wound became infected and Mistah Walt began to fail, she had been the first to sense the gravity of his condition. Without asking anyone's permission, she had gone to Chen Yu and returned to the apartment with the Chinese merchant's personal physician, who, she bluntly informed Allan, now was taking charge. As the Chinese doctor bowed politely to Allan and then crossed the living room toward the bedroom where Mistah Walt lay unconscious, Allan exploded.

"A Chinese doctor for my brother? That's ridiculous!"

"He is good doctor," Ming said stubbornly. "He is better doctor than yours."

"What do you know about doctors, you dumb Chinese whore?"

"No whore!" Ming cried in anguish, throwing herself upon Allan and pounding him furiously on the chest with her fists. "No whore! Love Mistah Walt! Love him! Love him!"

Seizing her wrists and freezing her into immobility, Allan stared down at her for several long, silent seconds. Then he said huskily, "By God, Ming, I believe you love him as much as I do. We'll give your doctor a try."

From that time on, Allan Randall had treated her with respect. But she no longer lived in his world.

Passing the mouth of a river joining the Snake from the Oregon shore and another from the Idaho shore, the party moved through increasingly difficult rapids into an ever-deepening canyon. Here and there, small groups of Chinese working river-level sandbars were encountered. Their returns so far had been meager, they told Ah Fat. Higher up the slopes, white men were working hard-rock claims, extracting ore from tunnels they had blasted into the canyon walls, some of the mines being small one- or two-man operations, others being worked on a larger scale.

One evening when the party was camped on a sandy flat on the Oregon side of the river near the largest mining operation they had yet seen, it was visited by two Chinese workmen and a white man named Barney Breen. Though she did not take part in the conversation, Ming heard enough of it to know that employment at day wages was being offered.

Ah Fat was wary. Mindful of the advice Chen Yu had given him and the warning of the Lewiston Chinese merchants that they should set up their own community, the headman temporized.

"We have come a long way and are tired," he said. "We wish to find a place to camp, unload our supplies, and build shelters. Then we shall decide whether we wish to work for ourselves or for you."

"Fair enough," Breen grunted. "There's a sandbar half a mile above here that might suit you. After you get settled, check back with me. I can put six of your men to work right away—maybe more later."

In talking to two Chinese laborers employed by the mining company, Ah Fat learned that they were well housed, fed, and paid, and were not mistreated by the white workmen. But since there were only five of them in the thirty-man crew, they did not threaten the livelihood of the American miners. Let another six to twelve Chinese be employed, serious causes for friction might arise. So for the time being, he thought it best to keep the party intact.

Half a mile upriver, next morning, the Chinese reached the spot that Ah Fat decided would be their home for the next six months. On the west side of the river, a bar of fine white sand topped with scattered clumps of bunch grass, low shrubs, and small trees stretched for several hundred yards parallel to the river. Behind the bar, benchland nestled against a steeply rising slope whose crest loomed four thousand feet above water level. Down this slope, cutting a deep "V" into it, tumbled a clear, cold, sparkling stream, which slackened into a series of pools as it crossed the bench and joined the Snake.

Looping down from the heights to the river, a trail wide enough for horses, pack animals, or cattle wound back and forth in a series of switchbacks, reaching water level near the upstream end of the sandbar. Though no human beings or animals were in sight this morning, the churned-up sand showed the trail to be frequently used. Here, the Snake could be crossed more easily than at any other point, for it was narrow, deep, and relatively quiet, with a favorable eddy setting from midstream toward the Idaho shore, where a low gravel bar offered an easy exit from the water. From that point, the trail wound up a gently sloping canyon.

Working from dawn till dark through the long summer days, the party built three low, windowless huts as shelters, carrying flat lava rocks from a nearby talus slide to a well-concealed ravine back away from the river and stacking them up in dry-wall fashion for the sides and backs of the huts, cutting saplings for roof beams, and thatching them with smaller limbs, grass, and turf. Supplies and tools were stored in one of the huts; the ten clansmen slept in the second; while the third was occupied by Ah Fat and Ming Sen.

As soon as the shelters were completed, the members of the party started panning for gold. Since most of their time in *Gum Shan* had been spent building railroads in the mountains and deserts of mining country, the Chinese were familiar with the tools of the prospector's trade—the shovel, the pick, the gold pan, the sluice box, the rocker—and adept at using the natural materials and forces at hand.

While half a dozen workers crouched hour after hour at the river's edge, patiently swishing water over sand in hand-held pans until a few golden flecks could be separated out, the others cut and shaped timbers, dammed the stream tumbling down from the heights, fashioned troughs to carry water to the sluice boxes, and began mining on a larger scale. Never having panned for gold before, Ming was excited by it, experiencing a delicious thrill as Ah Fat helped her pick out the golden flakes remaining in her pan.

"How much?" she asked breathlessly.

"Two-bits, maybe."

"But I worked all morning for that!" she cried in dismay.

"So you will work all afternoon for two-bits more," he said with a shrug. "Gold does not fall from the sky."

Since she was a woman, Ah Fat assigned her the task of

gathering wood for the cooking fire and preparing the meals. She also set and tended lines with which to catch fish for the party. At first she had little success, for it takes time to learn how to fish strange waters, but as the days passed her experiments with different kinds of baits suspended in pools and eddies at different depths began to produce a bountiful supply of trout, bass, catfish, and sturgeon, for the river in this sector abounded in fish.

Each morning and evening she went for a swim. Laughing at Ah Fat's warning that the currents and rapids below the sandbar were too dangerous to risk swimming, she slipped out of her clothes, dove into the cold water, and reveled in it as naturally and as unafraid as an otter.

At the lower end of the bar, a dark-brown lava rock the size of a house projected into the river, shielding a sheltered cove that could be reached only by a twisting path through a narrow crevice. Here, concealed from curious male eyes, Ming undressed and dressed before and after her swims, secure in the knowledge that none of the workmen in the camp could see her.

And here, one morning, she made a discovery.

Thinking that even in a river as swift and turbulent as the Snake there must be freshwater clams, mussels, or shrimp, she carried a sack and short-handled shovel as she made an exploratory dive downstream from the house-sized rock. In this quiet pool, the water was crystal clear and fifteen feet deep, moving slowly in a circular direction from the center of the river toward the western shore, eddying upstream, then out toward the main channel. As she had hoped, she found clinging to the rocks a number of dark crustaceans, which she scraped off and put into the sack. Swimming down to the bottom of the pool, she found an underwater bar of coarse white gravel lying below a flat lava ledge. Thinking there might be some clams buried in it, she scooped two shovelfuls of the gravel into the sack. With her lungs exhausted of air after a series of careful exhalations over a minute-long period, she headed for the surface.

The sun, which had just cleared the eastern rim of the canyon, felt good on her naked body. Letting it warm and dry her, she crouched at the river's edge as she rummaged through the material she had brought up from the pool. The mussels that she had scraped off the rock were small, but they looked edible. There were no clams in the coarse white gravel that she had shoveled into the bag, but as she sifted through it with her fingers her eyes caught a glint of sunlight on a tiny dull yellow crystal. At first, this did not excite her, for often the white sands of the bar were filled with flakes that looked like gold. But when put to the test of water and pan, they would prove to be as light as the sand itself, floating away over the rim of the gently rotated pan.

This crystal was different. No larger than a pinhead, it glowed rather than glittered, and as she stirred the palmful of gravel held in her left hand with the forefinger of her right hand, it showed a definite tendency to settle into the granules that surrounded it.

Her breathing quickened. Turning back to the pool, she cupped her hands like a gold pan, filled them with water, then cautiously rotated them as Ah Fat had taught her to do. During each rotation, she tilted her hands just enough to let the lighter materials wash out, while the heavier materials remained. After a while, only a small moist residue remained in her palm. Still there, clearly visible among the larger pieces of white gravel, was the tiny, dull yellow crystal. Carefully removing it with thumb and forefinger of her right hand, she put it between her teeth and bit down on it gently.

It had the softness of gold.

By now, the sun had dried her body. Quickly donning her black pantaloons, jacket, sandals, and wide-brimmed straw hat, she picked up the short-handled shovel and the sack containing the mussels and coarse white gravel, hurried along the twisting pathway that wound between the huge rock and the talus slide, and emerged at the lower end of the sandbar, where the Chinese miners were working.

Visitors were present, she observed with sudden alarm—

white men herding a band of horses and a dozen cattle. Apparently, they had just come down the steep trail from the western rim of the canyon, had seen the Chinese at work on the bar, and had paused to question them. There were four of them, Ming noted, and all of them were armed. As was her habit in the presence of white men, she let her slim, usually erect body sag into a round-shouldered slouch. Keeping her eyes fixed on the ground, she shuffled forward and joined the other Chinese workmen, who were bowing their heads in humble submission to the owners and masters of this country.

"Any of you Chinks speak English?" the leader of the four white men demanded harshly.

"I do," Ah Fat said, affecting a good humor Ming knew he did not feel. "I speak a little. What you want, Mistah Cowboy?"

"Hey, that's a dandy title for you, Frank!" one of the white men chuckled. "*Mister Cowboy!* Hell, you ain't punched a cow for wages since you growed up!"

"Shut up, Zeke! I'm tryin' to do some business with these yellow-bellies."

Letting his gaze run over the sandbar, the man noted the newly completed sluice box, the dam, the water troughs, and the three lava-walled huts set back in the ravine. His pale blue eyes returned to the headman.

"Quite a setup you got here. Findin' much gold?"

"We work very hard," Ah Fat answered, putting on his best simple-Chinaman, grinning-idiot look. "But we get only a little flour gold."

"How you fixed for food and supplies?"

"Got plenty lice. Got fish. Got tea."

"How'ja like to buy a fat steer for fifty bucks?"

"Oh, beef steer cost too much for poor Chinamen," Ah Fat exclaimed. Observing the man's scowl, he added hastily, "Maybeso we could buy side of pork for ten dollah and some fat hens for two dollah each."

"Can you pay in gold?"

"You bet—alla same Idaho price—fourteen dollah an ounce."

"Snake River flour gold ain't worth more than twelve."

"Okay—twelve dollah. You catchee side of pork and twelve fat hens?"

"Sure, we'll pick 'em up for you in Florence or Salmon City. We'll be comin' back this way in a week or so."

Watching the four white men herd the loose horses and cattle into the river, ride in after them, and make the crossing with an ease that bespoke long experience, Ming moved to Ah Fat's side. The grinning-idiot look had left his face; now it filled with alarm.

"Bandits!" he muttered. "Dogs of evil!"

"Why did you agree to buy food from them? We do not need it."

"We do not need their enmity, either. If we buy from them, perhaps they will do us no harm."

Lowering her voice so that the other Chinese workmen could not hear, Ming murmured, "I have found something of interest. Hold out your hand."

"Why?"

"Hold out your hand!"

Scowling at her, Ah Fat extended his right hand, palm up and open. Taking the crystal out of her mouth, where she had placed it for safekeeping, Ming put it in his palm.

"Look closely at this. Then tell me what it is."

He peered at the crystal, hefted it, rubbed it between forefinger and thumb, then tested it with his teeth. Though his face remained impassive, his eyes gleamed.

"It is gold!"

"You are sure?"

"Very sure. Where did you find it?"

"In a bed of white gravel at the bottom of a deep pool below the big rock. I have more of the gravel in my sack. Shall I get a gold pan and wash it?"

"No, not here!" he muttered, casting a quick look around. He picked up a gold pan, the sack, and the shovel, seized her arm and led her toward the lower end of the sandbar.

"Show me the place."

19

While Ming made dive after dive to the bottom of the pool downstream from the big lava rock, bringing up as much white gravel as she could carry each trip, Ah Fat squatted at the river's edge manipulating the gold pan. At the end of an hour's labor, he had recovered more coarse granules of gold, by weight, than the entire party of Chinese had panned and taken out of the sluice box during the three weeks it had been working the sandbar. As Ming lay panting from her exertions, Ah Fat gave her a questioning look.

"How long must you rest after each dive?"

"For three times as long as I have stayed under water. Otherwise, I would get cramps and drown."

"Could you teach the others to dive and work on the bottom as you do?"

"Never! They are afraid of water. Even if/they were not, it takes years of practice to become a good diver."

"Very well. You will work alone. For two hours each morning and afternoon, you will come here, dive, and bring up as much gold-bearing gravel as you can carry. Each afternoon, I shall come here and help you wash out the gold."

"Is what I have found of value?"

"Time will tell. But until we know, we will say nothing to the others." He looked at her sharply. "Do you hear me, woman? We will say nothing to the others."

"Yes," Ming said, nodding. "We will say nothing." A silence lay between them for a moment. Then she said softly, "You do not intend to share it with them?"

Ah Fat's face was stony. By strict rule, at the end of each day

the flakes of gold that the workers had gleaned from the pans
and sluice box were weighed, individually credited, pooled,
and then poured into a communal leather pouch, which the
headman concealed in a crevice between the rocks of the back
wall of the hut he and Ming shared. Ignorant and illiterate
though the Chinese laborers were, each man knew to a fraction
of an ounce what the results of his labors were each day. At the
end of the party's stay here, each man would know to the dollar
what his share of the total take should be. Unless he received
that exact amount, less expenses and a percentage to the
headman and the sponsoring company, he would protest long
and loud—and the elders of the Sam Yup Company would listen. Woe betide the headman who got caught cheating either
the workmen in his party or the company!

"For the present, we will keep the gold we find here separate from the rest," Ah Fat said. "After all, you are my wife.
You made the discovery. Your skill in working underwater is a
talent possessed by none of the others. So you should be entitled to a larger share than they."

"Who will decide that?"

"The ruling council of the Sam Yup Company."

"We will not see them for months."

"I know, woman, I *know!*" Ah Fat said angrily. Seizing her
shoulders, he squeezed down with his thick, powerful fingers,
an intensity in his voice that betrayed how deeply his greed
had been stirred. "When a strike as big as this one has been
made, no one can be trusted. Do you not understand that? We
must keep this to ourselves!"

Lowering her eyes, Ming nodded mutely. She understood
well enough. If she and Ah Fat succeeded in keeping her find
secret, they might become rich. If they failed, they might lose
both the gold and their lives. . . .

So far as Frank Vane was concerned, this last trip from Oregon to Idaho had hardly been worth the effort. Sure, the
horses and cattle they'd rounded up in the Wallowa Valley
had cost them nothing but a little risk and effort, so the five

hundred dollars they'd received for their sale had been pure
profit. But, hell, what was five hundred bucks after it was split
four ways?

Yeah, that fancy-pants Britisher who'd refused to let them
set up a tent saloon near his mine, who'd suckered him into a
prizefight whose rules he knew nothing about, who'd beaten
him on a fluke, and who'd got Zeke Hewitt, Matt LeCroix, and
Tom Crowell to think he was a great sport by buying up their
supply of booze for a good price, had contributed another six
hundred dollars to the kitty.

But, hell, that dough had been split four ways, too. Time a
man went on a spree in the Idaho mining settlements, with
eats, drinks, and a couple of nights with the girls, he was right
back where he started from—practically broke.

And hungover to boot.

Swimming their horses across the Snake to the head of the
sandbar where the Chinese were working, the four white men
found the straw-hatted, black-clad Orientals as humble and
submissive as they had been a week ago. Zeke Hewitt and
Matt LeCroix unloaded a gunny sack containing a side of
pork and two crates holding twelve live hens that the Chinese
had ordered. While Zeke and the headman haggled over the
amount of dust due, Frank Vane gazed contemptuously at the
foreigners.

Animals. That's all these stupid Chinks were. Living in
filthy hovels, rooting in the dirt like pigs, gabbling at one another in their crazy singsong lingo. Scavengers doing work no
white man would stoop to do, gleaning nickels and dimes
where white miners once had made dollars. Fawning, bowing,
groveling in disgusting servility before members of a superior
race. Vermin. That's what they were. Lice. Not fit to live in a
white man's country.

Still, if the amount of excavation and tailings was any
gauge, the twelve members of this party had been working
their butts off digging up the sandbar and the benchland
above it. They'd even dammed the creek and built a sluice
box. Been working here almost a month. Say each man

washed out a couple or so bucks' worth of gold each day. That'd mount up pretty fast. For the whole party, maybe two or three hundred dollars a week. Eight hundred to a thousand dollars a month. Say the party kept working the rest of the summer, fall, and winter—why, hell, this band of slant-eyes might stash away six or eight thousand dollars' worth of gold before next spring's high water flooded their diggings.

Now *that* would be a haul worth going after.

Watching the headman make a great show of difficulty in scraping up enough gold dust to pay for the side of pork and the twelve hens, Vane's eyes narrowed. Likely the Chinks would be real clever where they hid their gold. But the headman would know. He could be made to talk—if it came to that.

Though the transaction amounted to only thirty-four dollars, requiring less than three ounces of Snake River flour gold to be measured out on Zeke Hewitt's portable scales, the headman had to empty the pouches of two other Chinese workers, as well as his own, before a sufficient quantity of dust could be supplied. The pouches were suspended from leather thongs worn around each man's neck, Vane noted, and were carried on the chest under the quilted black cotton jackets. After Zeke Hewitt had agreed that the amount of dust was sufficient, the headman acted out a lugubrious pantomime demonstrating the emptiness of all three pouches, turning them upside down, shaking them, and then grinning dolefully.

"Alla same gold dust gone now! Poor Chinamen alla same broke!"

"Chinamen alla same goddam liars!" Frank Vane grunted. "If you ain't got no more gold than that, why have you stayed here a month?"

"Velly poor diggings," Ah Fat said earnestly. "Maybeso we move on soon."

"Yeah—and maybe you'll stay till next spring. My guess is, we'll see you again." He jerked his head at the others as he reined his horse around. "Come on, boys, let's go."

With Matt LeCroix and Tom Crowell following single file

and leading the pack horses, Frank Vane and Zeke Hewitt rode side by side as the trail slanted across the bench toward the steeply rising canyon wall. Hewitt gave him a crooked smile.

"Quite an act the yellow-bellies put on, wasn't it?"

"They didn't fool me none. My guess is they're doin' all right."

"Two, three bucks a day apiece?"

"At least that."

"I noticed they dammed the creek, built water troughs, and a sluice box. They wouldn't go to all that bother just for flour gold."

"My notion, too," Vane muttered, nodding. After a silence, he said, "Let's keep an eye on 'em for a week or so, without them knowin' it. Let's post a man with a pair of binoculars up on a high spot where he can see down into their camp without bein' seen himself—"

"Dead Sheep Point would be the spot for that. It's a thousand feet above the river, with a clear line of sight down the slope. From there, a man can see the whole length of the sandbar. He can even see down into the ravine where they've built their huts. Give him a good pair of glasses, he could count the lice in their pigtails."

"Okay, Zeke, that'll be your job. As soon as this trip is done, I want you to come back here and set your butt down on Dead Sheep Point with a pair of high-powered binoculars. Watch them Chinks from dawn till dark—"

"Alone?"

"Why not? It'll be easy work."

"Jesus, Frank, it'll be mighty dull and lonesome. Can't I have some company?"

"Sure. Who do you want—Matt or Tom?"

"Make it Matt. He don't snore as bad as Tom does."

"Just make sure neither one of you goes to sleep while you're behind them glasses," Vane said sharply. "I got a feelin' this bunch of yellow-bellies are into somethin' big. If they are, we'll let 'em pile up their hoard. Then we'll pay 'em a call. . . ."

20

Each morning, Ah Fat assigned the workers in the party their tasks for the day. Some dug, some panned, some chipped ore-bearing rock, some carried it to the sluice box, some worked the head gate, crushing box, recovery slats, or tailings pile. With typical Chinese thoroughness and frugality, he made sure that no square foot of accessible gold-bearing sand, gravel, or rock seam was overlooked in the party's search for the treasure that had drawn them to this distant land.

In order to make Ming Sen's assignment sound routine to the other workers, Ah Fat loudly instructed her to go to the lower end of the sandbar, after she had cooked and served the morning meal, and test the sand at the river's edge every three feet, down to and beyond the house-sized lava rock that projected out from the talus slope into the river. If she found a spot promising enough to work, he told her, she was to stay there until the time came in late afternoon for her to return to the living quarters, where she would prepare and serve the evening meal.

This gave her an opportunity to slip out of sight beyond the rock, disrobe, and commence diving. Since a three-foot-long rattlesnake once had been discovered coiled in the shade of a shrub at the foot of the slide, there was little likelihood that any of the other workers would wander beyond that point. If there was one thing this group of Chinese feared more than water, it was rattlers.

There had been some grumbling, this morning, when Ah Fat had assigned the chore of building a pen for the hens to Chea Sun and Chea Cheong, rather than to Ming Sen. Tending chickens was woman's work, they argued. True, Ah Fat replied, but pen building required a man's skilled hands and strong back, for the only materials available were rocks, bushes, saplings, and a few stunted pine trees.

"Build a good pen for the hens and Ming will reward us with a good meal," Ah Fat said good-humoredly. "Tomorrow we will have pork with our rice and fish. Next week, chicken."

By mid-morning, Ming was at work, diving. Toward the latter part of the afternoon, Ah Fat unobtrusively left the other workers, took the narrow path around the big lava rock, and found her squatting at the edge of the pool, intently peering down at the gold pan she was rotating in her hands. Noting that she was dressed and that the pile of white gravel beside her was not nearly as large as he had expected it to be, Ah Fat spoke to her angrily.

"Why have you stopped diving?"

"Because I am tired."

"This is all the gravel you have brought up today?"

"No, it is all that remains to be washed," Ming said calmly. Expertly tilting the gold pan so that the last of the water, sand, and gravel in it spilled out, she handed the pan to him with a smile. "Look."

The bottom of the pan, Ah Fat saw to his delight, was covered with granules of gold—an ounce, at least.

"Have there been many pans as good as this?" he asked.

"Most have been better," Ming answered. "You see, I have learned where the richer deposits lie, so I spend my time underwater working those ledges. It is very hard work, so I must stay above water longer. While I am resting, I separate out the gold, saving you that labor."

"Make sure you lose none of it," Ah Fat grumbled, though secretly he was pleased.

"This is what I have panned today," Ming said, handing him the leather pouch in which she had poured the results of her labors. "What would you judge its weight to be?"

"At least twelve ounces," Ah Fat murmured, his breathing quickening as he hefted the pouch. "Is there more gold-bearing gravel in the ledges?"

"A great deal more. And I will recover it much more quickly now that I know where it is."

Observing the way Ah Fat's hands cradled the pouch, tensing, relaxing, and then tensing again, Ming could guess what was running through his mind. Because he had married her at Chen Yu's insistence and her role in the party was primarily that of a boat handler and cook, she could not be expected to labor full time panning gold. Therefore, she was not entitled to an equal share in the gold recovered by the work party as a whole. Yet because of her diving skill, her find might prove to be much more valuable than theirs. Why should it be shared with them?

"This must be hidden," Ah Fat murmured. "If they find out we have it, they will insist on getting a major share. Then we will quarrel."

"Where will we hide it—in our hut?"

"No. That is the first place they would look."

"Here, under the big rock?"

"This is too close to camp," Ah Fat said, shaking his head. "Someone climbing the trail might see us working and sneak down to investigate when we are not here. We must find a hiding place that nobody but you and I could possibly locate."

Lost in thought, Ming was silent for a moment, then she said, "I know such a place."

"Where?"

"On the other side of the river. It is a cave with a well-concealed entrance. Since the workmen do not swim, they would never cross the river and go there."

"Can you swim across the river carrying a heavy pouch of gold?"

"Carrying ten heavy pouches of gold, I can swim across the river!" Ming said scornfully. "To a person skilled in water, the river offers no danger."

"You would be seen," Ah Fat objected. "The workmen would wonder why you are swimming to the other side."

"No one will see me. I shall wait until after dark."

"Exactly where is this cave? I must know."

Turning, Ming pointed at a spot on the Idaho side of the river several hundred feet above the level of the water. Extremely steep, the thousand-foot stretch of crumbled lava rock had over many eons of time split off from the higher basaltic palisades and tumbled down the slope until each rock had found its point of repose. Climbing such a jumble would be next to impossible, Ming told Ah Fat, for the sharp rock edges would cut a person's hands and feet to ribbons.

Halfway up the slope, projecting boldly out over the talus slide below, an immense black ledge overhung the jumble of broken rocks. Obviously part of the original lava flow that once had filled this sector of the canyon, it stood out like a reef in a rapid among the slide-rubble resting above, below, and around it.

"The cave entrance is under that projecting black ledge," Ming said. "It cannot be seen from here."

"How does one get to it?"

Draining out of the cave from a spring deep inside was a small stream, Ming said, which cut transversely across the mountainside. Where the trail to the Idaho settlements crossed that stream, a thick clump of bushes to the left of the trail screened a narrow, overgrown, long unused path worn by the pack animals of the prospectors who originally had dug into the cave for ore samples. All one need do was push through the bushes and follow the path to its end.

"Can you go to this spot after dark?" Ah Fat asked.

"Easily. Starlight is bright in the canyon."

"Will you not leave tracks that can be followed?"

"Did I not tell you that a small stream flows out of the cave?" Ming said impatiently. "It is shallow and swift, with a rocky bottom. I will walk in its bed. Five minutes after I have passed by, all traces of my footprints will be washed away."

Ah Fat nodded his satisfaction. "Very well. The cave under the overhanging rock shall be our hiding place." He gave her a quizzical look. "How did you happen to find it?"

Ming refilled her gold pan with gravel and lowered it into the water. "I was looking for berries in the thicket, found the little stream, and wondered where it came from. It led me to the cave."

Ah Fat appeared to accept that explanation, which relieved Ming, for it was only partially true. The complete truth was that she had been searching for a vantage point from which she could watch the activity of the big mining camp downriver; from that camp's vicinity the sound of blasting explosions could be heard periodically every day. On two occasions during the past month, she also had heard the exuberant *toot-toot, toot-toot* of the steam whistle and the *chug-whoosh, chug-whoosh* of its engine reverberating off the canyon walls as Allan Randall's small stern-wheeler, the *Hell's Angel*, fought its way up the river.

Because an intervening height of land blocked the sight line from the sandbar where the Chinese were working to the white men's mine half a mile downstream, Ming could not see what was going on there from the Oregon side of the river. But by crossing the Snake at the point where it customarily was swum by traffic from Oregon to Idaho, then climbing part way up the slope and moving laterally to the left downriver, she had hoped to get a view of the white men's camp without Ah Fat knowing what she was doing. This was important to her now. For she suddenly had realized that the hard-rock mine must be the one in which Allan Randall, Mistah Walt, and the Englishman who represented the British mining syndicate were interested.

After she had followed the little stream to its source, she was pleased to discover that from this vantage point she could indeed observe the mining camp downriver. From here, she also could see the *Hell's Angel*, which lay with its bow thrust into the sandbar on which the camp buildings sat. As she watched, puffs of black smoke belched from the boat's stack, two men got aboard, the landing plank and mooring lines were tossed on deck, the stern wheel started churning, and the boat swung out into the river.

Just below the sandbar on which the mining camp was located, the most violent, most feared rapid in this stretch of the

Snake churned and tossed. A month ago, the party of Chinese had been forced to unload and portage their boats' freight, then line the boats through the foaming white water one by one in two dawn-to-dark days of brutal, back-breaking effort. That a steamboat could negotiate the quarter-mile-long chute of tumultuous water seemed incredible to Ming. But somehow the *Hell's Angel* had accomplished that feat.

Longingly Ming gazed down the river until the small stern-wheeler moved around a bend in the steep-walled canyon and was lost from sight. Apparently the boat made the round trip from Lewiston every week or so, carrying mining equipment, workmen, and supplies. No doubt Mistah Walt had been aboard on some of these trips—and would be again.

What would she do if she saw him? She did not know. For the time being, she would be content just knowing that he was well—and nearby.

The rest lay in the laps of the gods.

21

Although Walt was appalled at the remoteness of the Golden Girl and the logistical problems involved in excavating, crushing, and smelting the ore, Lord Farley Windham Smythe appeared to be not in the least troubled by them. Yes, the lack of timber, roads, and level land in proximity to the mine was deucedly inconvenient, he admitted. But timber cut at a distance could be hauled in by wagon, pack animal, or boat. Trails, roads, and overhead tramways could be built. The stamp mill and smelter could be erected in such a way that they accommodated to even the steepest terrain.

"Have you considered building the stamp mill and smelter in a more readily accessible place?" Walt asked his brother. "Downriver, say, near Lewiston. You could transport ore to the site by boat."

"Handling costs would eat up all our profit," Allan said, shaking his head. "At the mine site, we can make money on eighty-dollar-a-ton ore. That's only five ounces of gold out of two thousand pounds of rock. Why pack all that waste rock downriver?"

"Can't your boat carry a hundred tons?"

"Sure. But with loading and unloading, a round trip between Lewiston and the mine would take at least three days. We'd have to handle the ore two extra times. Labor costs would kill us."

"But you own the *Angel,* so your transportation costs would be low," Walt persisted. "And you've told me that breaking down the stamp mill and the smelter equipment into loads that your boat can handle will take a lot of time and work. I'm wondering if the process can't be simplified."

"If you've no objection, Allan," Lord Smythe interjected pleasantly, "I'll attempt to explain the *modus operandi* we've decided to apply to the Golden Girl."

"Hop to it," Allan said. "I'm going up to the tunnel and see what's going on."

During the two days he stayed at the site, Walt came to appreciate the sharpness of Farley Smythe's intellect and the breadth of his experience in the field of hard-rock mining. Developing a prospect as big as this one required long-range planning, Lord Smythe pointed out. When completed, the eight-hundred-foot tunnel now being punched through the base of the basaltic spur would serve three purposes: adequate ventilation, exposure of the gold-bearing veins buried in the heart of the mountainside, and a supply of mineralized rock to be processed by the stamp mill and smelter.

"As soon as the tunnel is completed, we'll sink and drift both ways under the water level," he said. "We've already crosscut the pay streak on the hanging wall in six different places. We have enough ore-bearing rock accumulated to keep the mill and smelter busy for sixty days. By putting on a second shift, once the mill and smelter catch up, we'll be able to keep them going twenty-four hours a day."

"What will you fuel your boilers with?"

"Wood. Pine, fir, tamarack—they all burn well."

"There are no trees to speak of at water level," Walt said. "Where will you get your wood?"

"Up there," Lord Smythe answered, pointing a thumb at the canyon rim looming four thousand feet above the mine site. "We've laid out an eight-mile-long road up the side of the mountain and have started grading it. It should be finished in sixty days. Last week, we let a contract to a crew of cutters for one thousand cords of wood. It will be on hand when we need it."

Limestone rock for the mill and smelter foundations now was being blasted out a few miles downriver, Lord Smythe said; as soon as it had been hauled to the site, a pair of stone masons would start laying it. The steel bedplates for the mill would reach Lewiston from Portland within thirty days, Allan promised. If everything went as scheduled, the mine, stamp mill, and smelter would be in full production by the end of the summer.

"Sounds to me like you're going to need a lot bigger labor force than you've got now," Walt said.

"Oh, yes, we are!" Lord Smythe exclaimed. "In fact, that's one of our most pressing problems. We're counting on you to help us solve it."

"How?"

"You do legal work for a Chinese merchant in Portland, Allan tells me, who sponsors laborers brought in from Canton. The Chinese are excellent workers—"

"They certainly are," Walt interrupted curtly. "But mixing them with white workmen these days might buy you more trouble than you can handle."

"Oh, I'm sure our workmen will cause no difficulty," Lord Smythe murmured. He smiled at Allan, who had just rejoined them. "Ours is a jolly good crew, wouldn't you say?"

"Why shouldn't they be?" Allan said wryly. "They've got good wages, good food, good quarters, their own saloon—"

Walt frowned. "A saloon? Here in camp?"

"That's right—thanks to Farley. And a rip-snortin' prizefight every week, with their very own '*Champion of Hell's Canyon*' ready and willing to whip all comers—also thanks to Farley."

Looking sheepish, Lord Smythe muttered, "You've been talking to Barney Breen."

"I sure have. My God, Farley, what made you take on Frank Vane? He's twenty years younger than you are—"

"He challenged me. I had to respond."

"What would have happened if he had won?"

"I haven't the foggiest," Lord Smythe said with a shrug. "But he didn't. Now about those laborers we'll be needing. A dozen Chinese are camped on a sandbar half a mile upstream.

So far, Barney Breen hasn't been able to persuade them to come to work for us. Perhaps you could."

"When will you need them?"

"In three weeks."

"All right," Walt said. "Next trip upriver, I'll see what I can do."

During his stay in the Golden Girl camp, Walt heard the story of the prizefight many times and was amused by it. Obviously the miners thought Lord Smythe was quite a fellow. But Allan was concerned.

"Frank Vane and his crowd are bad news," he told Walt as they went aboard the *Hell's Angel* and prepared to head downriver. "I wish Farley hadn't antagonized them."

"Sounds to me like he handled them very well, buying their booze at a fair price after he'd whipped Vane. They must think he's quite a sport."

"You don't know them like I do," Allan said, shaking his head. "They're worthless scum. Matter of fact, Vane and Le-Croix worked for me when I first launched the *Angel*. They were so undependable I had to fire them. That night, they got drunk, came down to the dock, and tried to burn the boat."

"Did you have them arrested?"

"They left Lewiston before the law could catch up with them—with their butts full of birdshot." Allan grinned. "You see, I had a hunch they were going to try something nasty, so I slept aboard the *Angel*, with my shotgun near my bunk. When they lit their torches, I woke up and yelled at them. They ran like scared rabbits. I gave them twenty yards head start, then blasted them with both barrels."

"When did this happen?"

"A year ago. They left Lewiston two jumps ahead of the police, came upriver, and have been here ever since. If they ever get a chance to do me dirt, they'll jump at it. They're real bastards."

Directly below the sandbar upon which the mining camp was located, the river entered a narrow, sheer-walled canyon, its powerful current compressed into a series of whirlpools, eddies, troughs, and crests that turned the quarter-mile stretch of water downstream into one of the worst rapids in the river. Here, as at Wild Goose, Allan had implanted a deadman in solid rock, attached a length of steel-wire cable to it and to an empty barrel, and had used the steam-powered capstan to pull the *Angel* upstream. In this case, the deadman was secured in a rock located on the east side of the Snake, while the one at Wild Goose was imbedded in rock on the western shore.

"When you go through a rapid like this one," Walt asked curiously, "isn't there a danger of your paddle wheel fouling on the cable?"

"Practically none," Allan said, shaking his head. "Coming upstream, the cable is aboard and we keep it taut with the capstan. When we tie the barrel to it and turn it loose, most of its length sinks to the bottom of the river where it couldn't possibly foul the paddle wheel when we're going downstream."

Cocking his cap over his right eye, he rang for power, let the swift current move the boat out away from the sandbar, and then swung her bow downstream in a graceful arc.

"Of course, anything can happen to a riverboat if its pilot forgets the most important tool of the trade."

"Which is—?"

"The cap," Allan said solemnly, tapping his visor. "If it's cocked over the pilot's left eye, he knows he's going upstream. If it's over his right eye, he knows he's going downstream."

"What if it's setting square?"

"Then you're in for a bath, brother, because he doesn't know *which* way he's going. Hang on, Walt—the *Angel* wants to show you her style. . . ."

On his next trip upriver, Walt Randall paid a visit to the Chinese camp. Though Lord Smythe and Barney Breen offered to go with him, he thought it best that he go alone. Because of the intervening ridge, which must be climbed to an elevation of a thousand feet, then descended along the steep trail leading down to the river crossing, the traverse was too strenuous to be made on foot, Barney Breen said. So he saddled one of the small, hardy mules that was used to pull the ore cars and brought it to Walt, who regarded it skeptically.

"If that's the best you can do, Barney, I'd better walk."

"Oh, no, sir! This 'ere mule is a lot stouter than 'e looks. Treat 'im right an' 'e'll take you there an' back with no trouble at all."

"I've seen bigger Shetland ponies."

"Try 'im, sir. After pullin' ore cars, 'e'll think climbin' the ridge is a Sunday walk in the park."

Despite the fact that the stirrups almost touched the ground and the frail-looking mount appeared to weigh less than Walt did, the little mule moved up the slope at a strong, steady pace. Though it was not even breathing hard when it reached the crest of the ridge, Walt swung out of the saddle and let it pause a few minutes to rest. It promptly closed its eyes and fell asleep.

Far below, the river upstream from the ridge was in view, though from this height the figures working at the sluice box in the ravine, the ones panning sand along the water's edge, and the lone Chinese diving in the sheltered cove downstream from the sandbar looked more like insects than people. Except for the diver, who was naked, all the workmen wore straw hats, long-sleeved black shirts, and black pantaloons cut off between ankle and knee.

What industrious, persistent, patient people the Chinese were, Walt mused as he remounted the mule and rode down the twisting trail to the sandbar. This group had come upriver from Portland in three rowboats, Barney Breen said, lining the boats through the rapids with incredible effort, finding a gold-bearing sandbar long abandoned as unprofitable by white miners, building crude rock shelters, and working there from dawn till dark each day.

"If they clear two dollars a day apiece, I'd be surprised,"

Breen said. "Tell 'em if they go to work for us, we'll pay 'em four."

"Board and room included?"

"If it takes that to get 'em. We need workmen bad."

Reaching the foot of the trail, Walt rode toward a pair of slightly built Chinese who were wielding pickaxes against the wall of the ravine, while a large man, whose back was toward Walt, scolded them in Cantonese. Suddenly aware that a stranger was approaching, the two slim Chinese stopped working and cast frightened glances in Walt's direction. The bigger Oriental whirled around and stared at Walt. His mouth gaped open in surprise.

"Mistah Randall!"

"Ah Fat! What are you doing here?"

"Me boss work party. Honorable Chen Yu of Sam Yup Company tell us to go upriver till we find a place to dig gold. This is place we find."

"Well, I'll be damned! Is Ming with you?"

The look of consternation that had come to Ah Fat's face was gone now, dissolving into wariness.

"No, she not here," he said evasively. "Why you ask? You want her back?"

"Didn't she come upriver with you?"

"Oh, yes. But she not here in camp now."

"Where is she?"

"That way," Ah Fat said vaguely, gesturing downriver. "She go for swim just below big rock."

Remembering the lone figure he had seen in the sheltered cove from the heights, Walt scowled. "Isn't the river awfully dangerous to swim in? Aren't you afraid she'll be swept into the rapids and drown?"

"She swim like fish, Mistah Randall. Dive deep, swim long time underwater. Catch fish for supper. Catch shrimp and clam. You come to get her? You want to take her back?"

If only I could, Walt mused. *But it's not that simple.* Since she had left his household and cast her lot with a man of her own race, he could not lose face by showing undue concern for her welfare. After all, she was Ah Fat's wife now.

"No, I don't want to take her back," he said curtly. "I want to talk to you."

"I am honored. How can I serve you?"

"You know the big mine downriver?"

"Yes."

"It belongs to my brother. He's going to need more laborers in a couple of weeks. Barney Breen tells me he talked to you about your people working there."

"Ah, yes! We talked. He said he would pay each of us two-fifty a day."

"Not enough?"

"We wanted to try digging gold for ourselves."

"Having any luck?"

"We work very hard, Mistah Randall. Sometimes we make three dollar a day. Sometimes we make only two. But we have enough to eat. We have our own camp. We live in peace."

"Suppose we offered you four dollars a day? With room and board and a guarantee you wouldn't be molested thrown in?"

"Would be better. Much better."

"All right. Consider the offer made."

"We will think about it," Ah Fat said coldly. "Perhaps in a month or so—"

Realizing that the headman was rejecting the offer without appearing to do so, Walt said curtly, "Two weeks. We won't hold the jobs open any longer than that. Give my regards to Ming."

"You do not want to see her?" Ah Fat said, a leering smile on his face. "You do not want to talk to her?"

"All I want is for you to treat her with respect," Walt said harshly. "If you don't, I'll break your neck."

Mounting the little mule, he rode back over the ridge, feeling foolish for having let Ah Fat's crafty needling get under his skin.

"We Chinese are not as devious as we are made out to be,"

Chen Yu had said the night of the poker game before dealing the last hand. "But we do have a tendency to lay the solving of our problems in the laps of the gods. . . ."

All right, little tin god, Walt mused bitterly. *I'm laying my problem in your lap. Solve it if you can.* . . .

22

After three days of spying on the party of Chinamen panning gold on the Snake River sandbar, Zeke Hewitt and Matt Le-Croix were getting bored. Dead Sheep Point was hot, dusty, and dry, Hewitt mused disgustedly, and their camp nearby wasn't much better. Even taking two-hour turns with the binoculars between daylight and dark meant each man must put in a lot of time, for at this season of year dawn came early and sunset came late.

Hell of it was, Zeke Hewitt brooded as he relieved Matt LeCroix in mid-morning of the scorching summer day, there just wasn't much to see. A couple of Chinks digging into the base of the canyon wall. Another pair crushing rock with sledge hammers, putting it into a bucket suspended on a pole, carrying it over to a trough, and dumping it in. Downslope, still another Chink stirring the wet crushed rock with a shovel, lifting out the bigger pieces, patiently examining the riffles. Once a day, he would make a cleanup, emptying whatever precious metal he'd found into a buckskin pouch, but, try as he would, it had not been possible for Hewitt to make an accurate appraisal of the amount of gold the Chinese was recovering.

Spread out at regular intervals along the curving sandbar, Zeke Hewitt could see other yellow-bellies squatting on their heels like perched birds, patiently swishing sand and water around in their gold pans, painstakingly lifting out the few specks of color that remained when the bottom of their pan at last was almost empty. But here, too, it was impossible to tell how much gold they were recovering.

Comparing notes on what they observed, Hewitt and Le-Croix did establish a few interesting facts. An hour before dark each day the Chinks would stop working and check in with the headman one by one, transferring the contents of their pouches to his, being given in return a flat, round wooden marker about the size of a silver dollar, upon which the headman carved some sort of a symbol with a knife.

"He's givin' 'em credit for their dust," LeCroix muttered. "But the question is, how much?"

"I can't tell from here," Hewitt grumbled. "Two bucks worth of flour gold ain't enough to cover the little fingernail of a Chinese whore—"

"You should know," LeCroix said with a grin.

"Well, a Chinese girl sure beats them fat Indian squaws you go for."

"Hell, I like some meat on a woman, Zeke. Why, that Chink gal you had in Florence last trip couldn't have weighed a hundred pounds drippin' wet. A man could break her in two."

"That's what you think. Once she gets wound up, that little doll can turn a man every way but loose. And she's got a mighty tight mainspring. But gettin' back to the gold—where do you suppose the yellow-bellies hide it?"

"In the headman's hut, likely. It shouldn't be hard to find."

"They don't have no guns, so they can't put up much of a fight. What I'm wonderin' is, will it be worth the trouble?"

"That's for Frank Vane to decide. But I'll tell you this—I ain't gonna spend another winter in this neck of the woods. Soon as I get me some money, I'm headin' for San Francisco."

"Me too. This ain't my kind of country."

By the fourth day, the movements of the Chinese workmen on the sandbar below had fallen into such a set routine that Zeke Hewitt did not bother to raise the binoculars to his eyes except when a cleanup of the sluice box was being made or gold dust was being transferred from the pouch of a laborer to that of the headman. He did notice that at ten o'clock each morning one of the yellow-bellies would work for a time at the lower end of the sandbar, then take the twisting path that led between the foot of the talus slide and the house-sized lava rock, and disappear behind the rock downstream. At two o'clock, in the afternoon, Hewitt observed, the headman would do likewise. And at four o'clock, both the slim Chinese workman and the chunky, powerfully built headman would reappear and join the others, after which the slim workman would go to a shaded area near the lava-walled huts, build a fire, and start preparing the evening meal.

From Dead Sheep Point, Zeke Hewitt could not see the area downstream from the big rock. So on the fifth morning of his vigil—more out of boredom than interest—he moved several hundred yards along the descending trail to a switchback downriver from which he had a different angle of view. Here, concealed by several clumps of bunch grass growing along the trail's outer edge, he lay prone, steadied his elbows on the ground, and focused the high-powered binoculars on a small cove downstream from the big rock.

Nobody was visible there. He scowled. That was strange, for only minutes ago he had seen the Chink laborer move along the path between the slide and the rock. Since the sides of the cove were sheer, there was no place the yellow-belly could go—except into the river. Yeah, that's what the Chink must have done, for lying on the sand at the water's edge, Hewitt saw now, was a straw hat, a pair of sandals, a pair of black pantaloons, and a jacket. He'd gone for a swim, the rascal had. Stripped jaybird naked, dived in, and was still underwater. *Jesus!* Had the damn fool drowned?

Hearing the scuff of a boot on a rock, Zeke Hewitt looked up the trail in irritation as a dislodged pebble came bounding toward him.

"Hey, Matt! Watch where you're goin'!"

"What in the hell are you lookin' at?" Matt LeCroix demanded, scrambling down to join him.

"There's a Chink in that cove down yonder."

"Where?"

"Down there—now you can see him. He just come up."

"What is he doin'?"

"Looks like he's been diggin' underwater. He's got a short-handled shovel and a sack, and it looks like he's—" The binoculars suddenly shook in Zeke Hewitt's hands. "Christ-a-mighty! I don't believe it!"

"Don't believe what, Zeke? What's he doin'?"

"It ain't what he's doin'—it's what he is! Just *look!*"

"How can I, when you got the glasses?"

"He's a girl, that's what! And he's—she's, I mean—bare-assed naked!"

"Oh, hell, Zeke, you're crazy with the heat!" Matt LeCroix muttered. "Gimme them glasses . . . !"

When news of their discovery was relayed to Frank Vane two days later, he was more impressed by the description Zeke Hewitt and Matt LeCroix gave him of the manner in which the Chinese diver worked underwater than by the fact that she was a girl.

"She stayed under as long as two minutes, you say?"

"Yeah. We timed her."

"How much gravel did she bring up each trip?"

"A sackful. Ten, maybe twenty pounds."

"Coarse or fine?"

"Most of it was coarse. Like she'd dug it out of a ledge on the river bottom downstream from the big rock."

"When she washed it out, you could actually see gold nuggets in the bottom of her pan?"

"When he *looked* at the bottom of her pan, he could," Matt LeCroix said with a leer, nudging Zeke Hewitt in the ribs. "Only usually he was lookin' more at *her* bare bottom than at the pan's—"

"Well, what were *you* doin' when *you* had the glasses?" Hewitt demanded.

"Why, I was countin' the nuggets," LeCroix said solemnly. "And I seen a-plenty."

"Good-lookin' gal, is she?" Tom Crowell asked eagerly.

"You bet!" Hewitt exclaimed. "She's a real beauty!"

"If you like 'em yellow, skinny, and slant-eyed, like Zeke

does, she'll do," LeCroix said contemptuously. "But I wouldn't touch her with a ten-foot pole."

"Not if you could find a fat, greasy squaw, you wouldn't," Hewitt grunted. "You got no more notion of good tail—"

"Why don't you both shut up and let me do some thinkin'," Frank Vane cut in bluntly. "This could be a big haul."

A silence fell. Although Hewitt, LeCroix, and Crowell all had dabbled at prospecting in a small way, they knew that Frank Vane's knowledge of mining far exceeded theirs, for he had spent several years in placer and hard-rock diggings in many parts of the West. And he was well acquainted with the ways of the Chinese.

"When it comes to gold mining, the Chinks are mighty smart," Vane said thoughtfully. "These yellow-bellies knew exactly what they were lookin' for—a pocket deposited by a big eddy—"

"And they brought the girl along because she's an expert diver," Hewitt said.

"That's right. In China, they use women to dive for pearls. Probably use 'em for underwater minin', too. Anyhow, she seems to be bringin' up a lot of gold. Long as she keeps doin' it, we won't bother them Chinks. Matter of fact, it might pay us to get friendly with 'em."

"For how long?" LeCroix demanded impatiently.

"Till just before snow-fly."

"Then we hit 'em and git out of the country?" Tom Crowell said. "Is that the idea, Frank?"

"Yeah," Vane muttered. He was silent a moment, then added, "And maybe not *just* them."

Zeke Hewitt looked dubious. "Well, they ain't goin' to put up much of a fight, that's for sure. But they're bound to do a lot of squealin'—"

"Not if they're dead, they ain't," Vane grunted.

"You'd kill them all?"

"Why not?" Matt LeCroix said irritably. "Who's gonna miss a dozen yellow-bellies? For that matter, who's gonna know? All we got to do is dump their carcasses into the river and let 'em sink out of sight." LeCroix sneered at him. "Or are you too softhearted for that?"

"If it makes me some money and gets me out of this god-forsaken country, I ain't goin' to care a damn about a bunch of worthless Chinks," Hewitt said angrily. "But, damn it, somebody's bound to find out and set the law on our tail. It's a long, tough ride out of Hell's Canyon, with some mean mountains to cross 'fore we get in the clear. S'pose we get an early snowfall and can't get through the passes? What happens to us then?"

"You worry too much, Zeke," Frank Vane said coldly. "And you don't plan ahead."

"Have you figured out a quick getaway?"

"With no sweat at all. Just trust me."

"Well, you *are* the boss."

"Glad we agree on that."

"So what do we do for the next two months?" Tom Crowell asked. "Just sit on our butts and watch the Chinks?"

"First we round up another bunch of horses and cattle and take 'em to Idaho," Vane said. "We pick up some more pork and chickens for our yellow-belly friends. We make 'em a real good price, just to show 'em how friendly we are. Then we call on our fancy-pants British buddy, Farley Smythe."

"What for?" Matt LeCroix asked.

"Why, to let him know we got no hard feelin's against him," Frank Vane said with a thin-lipped smile. "After all, he whipped me fair and square and then bought our stuff." His smile faded. "Also, I'd like to get a close look at Allan Randall's pride and joy, the *Hell's Angel*. If we talk real nice to him, he might even take us for a ride. . . ."

By late September, the tunnel lacked only ten feet of being punched through the basaltic spur; the foundations for the mill and smelter had been laid; and all the boilers, stamps, bedplates, and heavy equipment had arrived in Lewiston. Each week, the *Hell's Angel*, laden with as much freight as she could carry, headed upstream for the Golden Girl camp.

As yet, the mine had not yielded a single dollar's worth of gold other than that taken from hand-sorted samples for assay purposes. Over a hundred men now were employed at the mine site and the woodcutters' camp. Payroll and expenses were running in excess of thirty thousand dollars a month. Yet despite the tremendous drain on capital and the lack of income from the mine, money from investors still was pouring in.

The day of reckoning would come late this fall, Walt Randall knew, after the mill and smelter got into full operation and the net yield of the mine could be compared to its gross cost to date. Personally, he was skeptical that the operation would show a profit its first year, if ever. But thanks to the long hours and hard work put in by the manager, bookkeeper, and attorney he had hired in Lewiston, an accurate accounting now could be made of every dollar that had been spent in developing the Golden Girl. So his own conscience was clear. As for Allan's conscience, it had never been in the least murky.

Climbing up to the pilothouse behind Allan as they prepared to head upriver shortly after dawn, Walt noted with disapproval the casual way his brother tossed the carpetbag containing a change of clothes, a quart of whisky, and a substantial amount of money into the corner. As the lines were cast off and the boat moved out into the river, he asked, "How much cash are you carrying this trip?"

"Thirty-five thousand dollars."

"Allan, it's ridiculous to pack that much money upriver each month. Can't you pay salaries and expenses by check?"

Allan shook his head. "Not a chance. Hell, Walt, at most mines the workmen are paid off every Saturday afternoon, go to town for a spree, and don't come back till Monday or Tuesday. We had a devil of a time hiring a crew that would agree to work a seven-day week with a payday only once a month."

"But you furnish the men free room and board. They even have their own saloon where they can charge their drinks. So they don't really need money. Why can't they endorse their checks and give them to you for deposit in a Lewiston bank?"

"Because they don't trust paper unless it's backed by the United States Treasury. They want cash."

"Well, it strikes me as a mighty poor business practice."

"Who ever told you mining was a business?" Allan said with a smile. "It's more like rolling dice or fighting a tiger." His face sobered as he gazed at the silvery surface of the river ahead. "Right now, I've got bigger worries than the money in that carpetbag. Like how much water will be rolling over the rocks at Wild Goose and Mountain Sheep rapids when the *Angel* tries to run them."

"Are we heavily loaded?"

"Right to the limit. With the water as low as it is, the *Angel's* bottom will clear the shelf at Wild Goose by a gnat's whisker, no more. Mountain Sheep may be too shallow to climb."

"In that case, what will we do?"

"We'll have to dump one of the boilers on a sandbar, then come back and get it later. Which will be a hell of a waste of time and labor. But I'm hoping we can squeak through. . . ."

23

Because of the cloud under which Frank Vane and Matt Le-
Croix had left Lewiston a year ago, Vane did not think it wise
for either of them to appear in the Golden Girl camp during
the two-day period each week when the *Hell's Angel* was tied
up to the sandbar. Not that he was afraid of Allan Randall.
But the bastard could be mighty touchy where his boat was
concerned. Since getting even with Randall for that birdshot
dusting in Lewiston would take some careful planning, Vane
intended to stay out of sight until the time came to act. But
Zeke Hewitt and Tom Crowell, posing as prizefight fans,
could and did go into the camp without arousing suspicion.

From the heights overlooking the site, Vane watched the
off-loading procedure every week, kept a close check on the
comings and goings of personnel, and began to formulate a
course of action.

As the river flowed, the Chinese camp and the Golden Girl
mine were only half a mile apart. Since the ridge between the
two camps rose steeply from water level, there was no easy,
direct route from one sandbar to the other. But by climbing a
thousand feet up the winding trail from the Chinese diggings,
a person could reach the lower section of the newly graded
road to the woodcutters' camp, from whence the descent to
the Golden Girl mine was easy.

By horseback at an unhurried walk, as Frank Vane timed it,
the distance could be traversed in twenty minutes.

Heavily laden as it was on its trips upriver now, the *Hell's
Angel* usually reached the Golden Girl camp in late afternoon,
tied up for the night, and did not begin unloading until the

next day. Secured to a deadman set in solid rock on the Idaho shore, a steel-wire cable led to the power capstan in the *Angel's* bow, a device which Vane knew was used to assist the boat in ascending the powerful, dangerous rapid just below the mining camp.

Invariably, the *Angel's* crew left the steel cable secured to the capstan and the deadman overnight as an extra mooring line. With the first light of dawn, next morning, a fresh fire was built under the boat's boiler, the crew went ashore and ate breakfast in the camp mess hall, then, with steam pressure up, the cable was slacked off, the barrel was tossed overside, the capstan was cleared, and the off-loading began.

This routine, too, was carefully noted by Vane.

Because of the weight of the equipment to be unloaded and the need to rig gin poles, skids, blocks, and tackle, it was usually mid-afternoon by the time the *Angel's* deck and hold had been cleared. Only then, if it happened to be a month-end payday, would the cash that Allan had brought upriver be sent ashore to the paymaster. Obviously, Allan did not want transportation out of Hell's Canyon available to workmen with money in their pockets. Even as the paymaster began to distribute the men's wages, the *Angel* would cast off her lines, give a couple of farewell toots of her whistle, and head downriver. Light, she drew less than a foot of water, Vane knew, and could bounce through the rapids like a cork. With a strong current behind her and Allan Randall's sure hands on the wheel, she would make the return trip to Lewiston in three hours.

Two months ago, Vane had asked Zeke Hewitt and Tom Crowell to keep their eyes and ears open for bits of information related to the progress of the tunnel, the size and location of the various crews, the amount of wages being paid the men, and the date and manner in which the wages and camp expenses were paid.

"Hell, Frank, are you thinkin' of goin' to work at an *honest* job?" Zeke Hewitt kidded him. "That'll be the day!"

"Just get me the dope, Zeke," Vane said stiffly. "When the time comes, I'll tell you what I'm thinkin'."

Despite a number of visits to the Chinese camp and a continuing surveillance of the sandbar, Vane found it difficult to estimate how much gold the yellow-bellies were recovering. But he made a well-reasoned guess. Knowing this type of mining as he did, he felt that the five Chinks panning the bar would be lucky to clear three dollars a day apiece. If they averaged that for the three months they'd been working the sandbar, their take by the end of September would be fourteen hundred dollars.

From the way the five other yellow-bellies hacking at the canyon wall and working the sluice box kept at it, they must be doing somewhat better. In all probability, they had hit a surface outcropping of a pinched or fractured vein that was yielding enough gold to convince the headman, who checked their cleanup once a day, that it was more profitable to keep them chipping away at the hard-rock operation than having them labor at the river's edge with pans. Say each of them had recovered eight dollars a day. Their take by now would total thirty-six hundred dollars.

The part of the Chinese activity that most intrigued Vane was the underwater work of the girl diver. Twenty-five years ago, he knew, two distinct gold strikes had been made in Idaho Territory a hundred miles east of Hell's Canyon. On the North Fork of the Clearwater, the gold had been very fine; thus, the district had been called *Orofino*. On the South Fork of the Clearwater, the gold had been very coarse; thus, the district had been named *Orogrande*. Until now, all the gold recovered from the sandbars on the Snake had been of the fine-grained variety, yielding returns so meager that few white men bothered to work them.

But a freak deposit could occur anywhere. Whether the Chinese had struck a continuation of the rich vein that honeycombed the nearby Golden Girl mine or had located a water-deposited pocket brought downriver many years ago, did not really matter. The fact that the girl had continued to work the ledge four hours a day for three months, with what appeared to be excellent results, must mean that the treasure she was recovering was substantial.

How substantial? Well, in that kind of gravel in the Oro-grande district, fifty-dollar pans had been commonplace. Say she averaged ten such pans a day. That would be five hundred dollars for a day's work. In ninety days, she would have recovered forty-five thousand dollars' worth of gold.

There, Vane brooded exultantly, was a hoard worth going after!

Now in this final week of September, autumn's first early snowfall had dusted the nine-thousand-foot peaks of the Seven Devils Mountains, which guarded the Idaho side of Hell's Canyon, and the ten-thousand-foot crests of the Wallowa Mountains, which looked down on the Snake River from the Oregon side. Camped near the Chinese diggings one evening on a return trip from Idaho, Frank Vane decided that the time had come to reveal his plans to his three companions.

Figuring that they would need a bracer, he uncorked a quart of whisky and poured drinks around. When they all had wet their whistles, he said, "It's time to make our move."

"Against the Chinks?" Matt LeCroix said.

"Yeah."

"How much gold do you figure they've stashed away?" Zeke Hewitt asked.

"At a rough guess, fifty thousand dollars."

"Lord-a-mighty!" Tom Crowell chortled. "Won't we have us a time in San Francisco on that kind of money!"

"When do we hit 'em?" LeCroix asked.

"The morning after Allan Randall's boat makes its next trip upriver. Way I figure, that'll be day after tomorrow."

"What's the *Hell's Angel* got to do with us hittin' the Chinks?" Matt LeCroix asked with a scowl.

Not answering for a time, Vane picked up the bottle, refilled the empty cups, took a healthy swallow of whisky, and then gave LeCroix a thin-lipped smile.

"Still got a few pellets of birdshot in your butt, Matt?"

"Yeah—and they itch like hell."

"Still like to get even with Allan Randall for what he done to us?"

"You bet I would!"

"Still remember how to fire the boiler and operate the engine room controls of the *Angel,* like you done for a spell before Randall gave us the boot and ran us out of Lewiston?"

"As you damn well know, Frank, I was just as good a fireman as you were a deckhand," LeCroix exclaimed angrily. "If that bastard Randall hadn't canned us, we'd be workin' now at good wages as second engineer and assistant pilot on a riverboat somewhere. But you ain't answered my question. What's the *Hell's Angel* got to do with us hittin' them Chinks?"

"Well, for one thing, the *Angel* will be carryin' at least thirty thousand dollars in cash to meet the Golden Girl's monthly payroll," Vane said quietly. "For another, she'll give us a fast ride out of Hell's Canyon."

"How will she do that?" Tom Crowell demanded. "Are you figurin' on stealin' her?"

"I sure am," Vane said with a grim-faced nod. "If we time it right, the *Angel* will be waitin' for us with steam up, no crew aboard, the money in the pilothouse, and nobody able to keep us from castin' off and headin' downriver. Now listen close. Here's what we'll have to do. . . ."

24

Ming Sen was so tired these days that her health was beginning to suffer. Try as she would, she could not convince Ah Fat that diving was extremely exhausting work that built up poisons in the blood and ill-humors in the lungs that only time and adequate rest could alleviate. From the beginning, she had known that he had a brutal streak in his nature. He had also proven to be a greedy, suspicious man, who, despite the great value of the gold she gave him each day, kept demanding more, mistrusted her despite her complete honesty with him, and was becoming increasingly apprehensive as the treasure he was concealing from the other Chinese grew in worth.

Indeed, he had reason to be apprehensive, Ming brooded as she rose in the pale gray light of dawn that late September morning, built a small cooking fire outside the lava-walled huts, and started heating up the rice-fish-pork gruel and tea that she would serve Ah Fat and the crew of laborers for their breakfast. While the amount of gold recovered by the Chinese workmen had been somewhat greater than expected, her own find had proved to be ten times more valuable than that of all the others combined.

With her help, the secret of that find had been successfully concealed from the others. It had also been kept from the four evil-looking American bandits who rode through the camp every week or two, trying to ingratiate themselves with the Chinese by selling them pork and poultry at low prices, while it was obvious from their furtive glances around the sandbar that their real interest was in what they could steal.

Ming suspected that when high water came next spring, forcing Ah Fat and his party of laborers to leave Hell's Canyon and return to Portland, the headman might even risk concealing the find from Chen Yu and the elders of the Sam Yup Company. This would be a capital offense, of course, for which he would lose his head, if discovered. But who could bear witness against him? Only Ming Sen herself. So now he was watching her closely—just as she was watching him.

In Japan, Ming knew, certain fishermen trained a pelican-like bird to dive and bring up fish, the bird being prevented from eating its catch by a cord noosed around its neck that could be tightened by its master so that the bird could not swallow. Ah Fat was exercising the same kind of control over her, using her diving ability for his own personal gain. Since her knowledge of the secret hoard of gold could cost him his life, he would not hesitate to take drastic means to silence her if he did decide to risk keeping the gold for himself.

Twice a week she swam across the river and deposited another buckskin pouch of gold in the cave under the big projecting rock. Waiting until the Chinese laborers fell asleep, she slipped out of the hut she shared with Ah Fat, went down to the river's edge, took off her sandals, and tied them around her neck. Though she preferred to swim naked, she knew that her light-colored body would be more visible in the dark, so she did not disrobe, tightly belting her quilted black jacket over her black pantaloons at the waist so that its fullness would not impede her movements. Easing into the cool water with not even the tiniest splash, she angled her slim body upstream into the current, letting it thrust her toward the far shore, swimming with minimal effort, not fighting the great strength of the river but becoming a part of it.

Once across, she put on her sandals, followed the trail up the slope to where the creek crossed it, turned left through the screen of bushes, then, wading in the creek so that her footprints soon would be washed away, ascended it to the cave. At this time of year, the sky was cloudless and myriad stars hanging low over the canyon gave her all the light she needed to see her way. After she had deposited the pouch of gold in its hiding place well within the cave, she returned to the hut, changed into dry clothes, and fell into an exhausted sleep.

Before consenting to use the cave as a secret repository for the gold, Ah Fat had insisted on seeing it for himself. Ostensibly going on a berry-picking trip to the Idaho side of the river, he and Ming had taken a boat one afternoon, rowed across the Snake, and climbed the trail and the creek bed to the cave, taking great care not to be seen by the workers on the sandbar. Ah Fat had been favorably impressed with the hiding place.

"This is a good spot, which shall be known only to you and me," he said. "You will bring all the gold you find in the pool here. It is better that the others do not know about it until the elders of the Sam Yup Company decide how it is to be distributed. Before we return to Portland next spring, we will devise a way to conceal it with our supplies in the boats."

"If the ledge continues to be rich, it will be very heavy," Ming warned him.

"I know. But since you do the cooking, no one will think it unusual that you insist on handling the sacks of rice and tins of tea. It should not be difficult to hide a few pouches of gold on the bottom of each sack and tin."

No, it would not be difficult to do that, Ming brooded as the cache of gold grew. Nor would it be difficult for Ah Fat to arrange a fatal accident for her, once her usefulness to him was done. For that matter, he could kill her as she slept, if he chose to do so, without arousing any protest from the Chinese workmen, to whom the life of a young woman of Ming's class was worth little. But she doubted that he would dispose of her so openly, for Chen Yu had made it clear to him that she had special status with the American attorney who represented Chinese interests in Portland. Since Chen Yu would lose face with Mistah Walt if Ah Fat deliberately mistreated her, it was not likely that the headman would risk his anger. But an accident for which no blame could be placed would be another matter.

The sky above the canyon was brightening now with the full light of day, though the shadows cast over the sandbar by the looming heights to the east would linger far into the morning. The Chinese workmen were beginning to stir, coming out of the hut in which they had slept, stretching, yawning, making jokes with one another as they washed their faces and hands in the stream tumbling down the mountainside. Ah Fat was the first to squat beside the cooking fire as she filled wooden bowls with food and cups with tea.

"You were not seen last night?" he asked in a low voice.

"No. Nor was I heard."

"You left your wet clothes on the roof of our hut. The men may see them and wonder."

"That a woman should wash her clothes will cause men as dirty as they to wonder? They should do some washing, too!"

"Quiet, woman!" Ah Fat said sharply. "I will not permit you to argue with me."

Falling silent as Kong Mun Kow, Chea Lin Chung, Chea Chow, and the others approached the fire, squatted, and accepted bowls, Ming did not demean Ah Fat by open dispute. But inwardly she was seething. He would not permit her to argue with him! No. But he would permit her to begin each day by rising at dawn, building a fire, and preparing a meal for twelve people. After breakfast, he would permit her to clean up the bowls, chopsticks, teapot, cups, and pots, feed the hens, chop up the meat for the evening meal, and put the rice to soaking.

Following these chores, he would permit her to take shovel, sack, and pan, make her way to the pool downstream from the big lava rock, and spend four exhausting hours diving, digging, and bringing up gold-bearing gravel. Then he would permit her to spend another two hours panning out that gravel, after which he would permit her to return to camp and cook the evening meal. Twice a week, after he and the others fell asleep, he would permit her to swim across the river, hide the gold in the cave, swim back, and then sleep for a meager five hours before rising and engaging in the same strength-sapping routine again.

If only he would show a little gratitude or appreciation for what she was doing, she would not mind so much, Ming brooded as she served Chea Chow, Chea Ling, and Chea Cheong. Instead, his treatment of her grew more callous every day. Was he hoping she would work herself into such a state of exhaustion that she would sicken and die? If that happened, he could tell Chen Yu that she had been too delicate to endure the privations into which Chen himself had sent her. Thus, no fault could be laid on Ah Fat for her death.

If that were his game, Ming mused angrily as she dished up gruel and poured tea for Chea Sun, Chea Yow, Chea Shun, and Chea Po, he was going to get a surprise. Because she was not delicate. She was as hard as nails. Furthermore, she knew now what she must do.

She must tell Mistah Walt about the gold.

On several occasions during the past two months, she had swum across the river during daylight hours, scrambled through the rocks that covered the steep slope below the cave, and reached a vantage point part way up from which she could see the landing where the *Hell's Angel* tied up on its weekly trip to the Golden Girl mine. Twice, Mistah Walt had been aboard—and her heart had nearly burst in her breast as she watched him walk ashore. She had wanted to cry out to him. She had wanted to go to him. But she knew she dared not—for it had been for the welfare of his career that she had left him and become Ah Fat's woman.

Ah Fat's woman? *No! His wife!* Mistah Walt himself had given the headman the stern warning: "By the laws of this country, you will be Ming's husband and she will be your wife. If you mistreat her, the law will arrest you—and chop off your head!"

Later, Ah Fat had laughed and boasted to Ming that the laws and marriage ceremonies of this country meant nothing to him. But when he learned that the American magistrate who had given him the warning was close at hand, he would not laugh. Indeed, when Ming told him that she had revealed the secret of the hidden gold to Mistah Walt, the headman would turn pale and quake with fear, for he would realize that his fate now lay in her hands.

That thought pleased Ming.

She would not accuse Ah Fat of attempting to keep the gold for himself, she mused. No, she would say he had told her he fully intended to reveal the find to the elders of the Sam Yup Company, so that they could determine its fair distribution. Once she did that, he would not dare harm her, just as he would not dare risk keeping the gold. He would hate her for what she had done, of course. But that would be of no consequence, for once Mistah Walt knew the role she had played in finding and developing the underwater ledge she would gain much face with him and Chen Yu and would forever be safe from vengeance by Ah Fat.

It would not be difficult to get word to Mistah Walt, Ming brooded as she ate her own meager breakfast. Yesterday afternoon she had heard the whistle of the *Hell's Angel* reverberating off the walls of the canyon as Allan Randall announced the boat's arrival in his usual exuberant style, the sound soft and muffled at first because of the narrowness and crookedness of the canyon, then growing in volume as the steep walls on either side threw back and amplified the sound, until here, half a mile upstream, its volume was much louder than at its source. Mistah Walt probably would be aboard. Even if he were not, she trusted Allan well enough to give him a message to his brother.

Their breakfast done, the workmen rose and went about their labors, getting sledge hammers, shovels, picks, and pans out of the supply hut in which Ah Fat insisted they be stored each night, and then moving to their assigned tasks for the day.

As soon as she had finished her camp chores, Ming mused as she gathered up the empty bowls and cups, she would go to the pool downstream from the big lava rock. But instead of disrobing and diving for gravel, she would slip into the river fully clothed, swim underwater until well past the bend, then surface and let the swift current carry her downstream to the sandbar below the Golden Girl camp. It would be dangerous, for this was a narrow, turbulent stretch, filled with rapids, whirlpools, slicks, and eddies that could drown even a skilled swimmer. But at this time of year, the Snake River was running at its lowest stage, she had come to know its hazards well, and the prospect of seeing Mistah Walt again so delighted her that the risk seemed well worth taking.

How surprised he will be! Ming thought happily as she scrubbed the bowls with sand, then carried them down to the stream and began washing them. *I will come up out of the river like a mermaid. I will bow to him. He will stare at me, unable to believe his eyes. I will smile and say . . .*

The sharp, metallic sound of shod hoofs striking loose rocks made Ming whirl around and glance upward. Seeing four riders moving down the steep, winding trail above the sandbar, she knew at once who they were. She leaped to her feet, ran to the hut she and Ah Fat shared, donned her straw hat, pulled it well down over her face, then scurried back to the stream and resumed her cleanup duties. Though the four American bandits had behaved well enough during their recent visits to the camp, she was not going to risk mistreatment by letting them learn that she was a woman.

Out of the corner of her eye, she watched as the horses of the four white men negotiated the final switchback a hundred feet above the sandbar, turned toward the camp, and broke into a run. It struck her as strange that the men should be in such a hurry. Also odd was the fact that no loose horses, cattle, or pack animals were with the four riders this trip. Strangest of all was the fact that in the right hand of each man, held down against the side of his horse as if to be concealed until the last instant, was some sort of tool—

"Go git 'em, boys!" the bandit leader shouted harshly. "Just remember—the headman is mine!"

"And the gal belongs to me!" yelled the bandit riding behind him.

"Hooeey, gents, it's Chink-butcherin' time!" cried the third
bandit. "Pay no mind to their squeals!"

Frozen with horror, Ming saw the four riders raise their
right hands. Each held a double-bitted axe, the heads gleaming with recent honing. During the several seconds she remained motionless, every detail of the scene in the dawn-
shadowed canyon etched itself indelibly into her mind, like
the stylized staging of a Chinese play whose violence is so ex-
aggerated that it cannot be regarded as real.

Crouched by the river's edge with their gold pans, five of
the Chinese workmen stared up at the axe-wielding horseman
riding toward them in paralyzed disbelief. In the pocket
against the canyon wall, at the base of the sluice box, at its
head gate, and at the crushing box, Ah Fat and the other five
Chinese cast panic-stricken looks at the two riders coming toward them, unable to move. Like chickens struck motionless
by the sudden shadow of a diving hawk, they stood defenseless and helpless as the deadly axes rose and fell.

Suddenly Ming no longer saw what was happening to the
others. For the fourth rider was bearing down on her.

Hypnotized by the gleaming blade of the axe he was carrying, she did not move quickly enough to avoid his grasp as he
reached down, seized her by the throat, and swung off his
horse. Dropping the axe and letting the horse run free, he
took hold of the front of her jacket and ripped it open, expos-
ing her naked breasts.

"Got you, you little bitch!" he grunted triumphantly.
Releasing his grip on her throat with his left hand, he put his
arms around her and brutally pulled her body against his.
"Now we'll have some fun!"

She stiffened herself against him. But resistance was useless;
he was far too strong for her. As he bent her backward and
ground his body against hers, she could hear the Chinese at
the river's edge screaming in\mortal terror as the axe-wielding
rider methodically chopped them down. Over by the sluice

box, one of the white men had dismounted and was grappling with Ah Fat, who, more quick-witted and less intimidated than the others, had seized the bandit leader's axe and wrested it out of his hands. The headman raised the axe to strike.

"Hit him, Matt!" the bandit leader shouted hoarsely.

Using skills taught her long ago, Ming suddenly ceased resisting, sagged against her attacker as if willing to do whatever he desired, and collapsed to the ground. With a snort of satisfaction, he fell clumsily on top of her, eased his grip on her back with his left hand and reached down for the waistband of her pantaloons with his right hand.

Like an eel, she squirmed out from under him. Chopping sharply down on the nape of his neck with the edge of her open left hand, she stunned him just long enough to permit her to leap to her feet, cast a quick look around, and decide upon the only possible course of action that could save her.

A pistol roared, the sound echoing back and forth in the confines of the narrow canyon.

"Got him, Frank!" cried the mounted bandit near the sluice box.

Struck squarely in the face by the bullet, Ah Fat crumpled and fell.

"You dumb bastard!" the bandit leader shouted angrily. "I said hit him—not shoot him!"

To the other Chinese, water was an element to be feared, thus the five men cowering at the river's edge had made no attempt to leave the sandbar. But to Ming, water meant safety.

Turning, she ran toward the deep, swirling eddy at the head of the sandbar where Idaho-bound travelers and animals customarily swam the Snake, and dived in. By the time she surfaced, she was behind a rock which jutted out into the river from the Idaho shore, well hidden from the four American bandits on the sandbar.

Lying still as a frightened muskrat, with only her eyes and nose above water, she breathed deeply for several minutes while her heartbeat slowed, her strength returned, and her mind examined her prospects.

Ah Fat and the ten Chinese laborers all were dead, she knew, chopped down in an attack so sudden and treacherous that only the headman had put up any resistance. From the way the leader of the bandits was cursing two members of his band, Ming gathered that he had intended to keep Ah Fat alive until he could be tortured into revealing the hiding place of the party's gold. She, too, was to have been captured rather than killed, she guessed, though how they had known she was a woman puzzled her. She heard the man who had attacked her shouting angrily at the bandit leader.

"Sure, she got away! But don't blame me! She just slipped out of my hands. Goddam it, Frank, did you ever try to hang onto a wet fish—?"

"Wet fish, hell! If you'd tied her up like I told you to do instead of tryin' to pull her pants off, she wouldn't have gotten loose!"

"Well, you didn't do so good yourself, lettin' that headman take your axe—"

"He caught me off balance, damn it! Then you, Matt—you had to go and shoot him!"

"What was I s'posed to do? Let him cut your head off?"

"You could have knocked him down with the barrel of your pistol, couldn't you?"

"And him about to swing that axe? No way was I gonna go near him, Frank."

"Well, there's no sense bitchin' about it," the bandit leader grunted. "Whatever gold the Chinks have got stashed away is bound to be hid in the walls of them huts. Let's tear into 'em."

As the men started to move toward the huts, the bandit who had attacked Ming turned toward the river and stared at the spot where she had dived into the water. The leader looked at him sourly.

"Somethin' wrong, Zeke?"

"Yeah. I keep thinkin' about that girl."

"That's your trouble. You're always thinkin' about that girl."

"I'll bet she's still alive, Frank. The way she can stay under-water, she could've swum clean over to the other side of the river without us seein' her. She could be hidin' in the rocks over there right now, watchin' us—"

"What if she is?"

"Well, I was thinkin' maybe I should cross the river and look for her. If I find her, I'll bet I can make her tell us where that gold is stashed away—even if she don't speak English."

"Forget it, Zeke. The Snake is a mighty nasty river to swim. Scared as she was, she probably got swept into a whirlpool and drowned. Anyhow, we ain't got no time to spare if we're gonna get that payroll and take that boat."

"That's so, I reckon."

"C'mon—give us a hand tearin' into them huts."

With the four bandits occupied ripping off the flimsy roofs and prying into the loosely laid rock walls of the huts, which were some distance removed from the river, Ming Sen climbed out of the water, ascended the trail to the spot where the stream crossed it, turned left through the screen of bushes, and made her way to the cave in which the gold was hidden.

She felt safe here. From the cave's well-concealed mouth, she could see the sandbar on the opposite side of the river and the bloody, mutilated bodies strewn along its edge. She could see the trail down which the bandits had ridden. The landing to which the *Hell's Angel* now was moored also was visible from this spot. She could see black plumes of smoke rising into the still early morning air from the boat's stack, and she knew that a fire had just been built under the boat's boiler.

She was puzzled. Had the bandits observed her at work in the pool downstream from the big lava rock? Did they know the value of the find whose secret she had shared with Ah Fat? Apparently, they did. Perhaps they even suspected that she and Ah Fat had concealed the find from the other Chinese and had hidden that portion of the gold in a place separate from the community hoard. But they could not know that the separate place was on the Idaho side of the river.

A perverse thought struck her. Half an hour ago, by the

laws of this country, she had been Ah Fat's wife. Now, by those same laws, she was his widow. Which meant that she was free. And hidden in the cave behind her was fifty thousand dollars' worth of gold whose existence was known only to her.

She wondered what Mistah Walt's reaction would be to that piece of information.

That death in its most violent form had come to eleven of her countrymen in the depths of this remote canyon half a world away from the South China province in which they had been born, did not affect her unduly. Here, as in China, violent death was commonplace, she had learned. She had survived; that was all that mattered. And if she kept her wits about her, she soon would be reunited with the man who had taught her the meaning of happiness and love.

25

Half an hour's work with pick, sledge hammer, and shovel had exposed every possible nook and cranny in which pouches of gold could be hidden. Ordering the other three men to cease their labors, Frank Vane stared bitterly down at the twelve partially filled buckskin sacks that had been found concealed in crevices in the back wall of the headman's hut. He guessed that each contained thirty to forty ounces of gold.

"You reckon that's all of it?" Zeke Hewitt asked, hunkering down beside him.

"I reckon that's all we're gonna find," Vane grunted.

"What'll it amount to?" Tom Crowell inquired.

"About five thousand dollars."

"Jesus Christ, Frank!" Matt LeCroix exclaimed in disgust. "You said they'd have at least fifty thousand bucks stashed away!"

"What I said, you stupid son of a bitch, was that the Chinks workin' the sandbar would have around five thousand dollars. And that's what we've found. It was the girl and the headman who'd made the big strike, I told you. From the way they acted, I figured they were keepin' it to themselves and hidin' it in a special place. Which was why I wanted to keep them alive. But Zeke got so horny he forgot what he was s'posed to do and let the girl get away. And you got so trigger-happy you shot the headman—"

"If I hadn't shot him, he'd have split you wide open," Le-Croix muttered. "Maybe I should have let him."

"Why argue about who should have done what?" Tom Crowell said impatiently. "It's the gold that matters. Since it ain't in the huts, where do you suppose they hid it?"

"Under a rock, probably," Vane answered sardonically. Carrying the pouches over to his horse, he put them away in the saddlebags, then turned and made an angry gesture that embraced the entire area. "There can't be more than a million of 'em in this goddam canyon. All you got to do is find the right one."

"Hell, Frank, we ain't got time to go lookin' under rocks," Zeke Hewitt protested. "Not if we're goin' after that boat and the payroll."

"Zeke's right," LeCroix said. "Wherever that gold is hid, it ain't gonna melt. We can come back and look for it later—in a year or two, say. But we know where the payroll is. That's thirty thousand dollars in easy-to-carry cash. I say let's go after it, take the boat, and get the hell out of here."

"I'm for that," Vane said grimly. "But before we go, there's a chore we'd better do."

"What's that?" Hewitt demanded.

"Get rid of these bodies."

"You mean *bury* 'em?" Hewitt said, his face contorting with distaste. "That'll take a lot of diggin', Frank."

"No, it won't. All we got to do is get them boats the Chinks brought upriver, chop holes in their bottoms, dump in the bodies, and then pile rocks on top of 'em. That way, when we push the boats out into the river, they'll fill with water and sink."

"By God, that's a good idea!" Hewitt agreed. "With the Chinks and their boats gone, who's gonna know they didn't just pull up and leave? But there's one other thing we ought to do, Frank."

"What's that?"

"Throw their tools and supplies in the river, too. That way, it'll really look like they broke up camp and left."

"All right," Vane said. "Let's get at it. When we've finished, we'll ride over the ridge to the Golden Girl camp. Our timing should be about right. . . ."

Because of the size of the crew now working at the Golden Girl, breakfast was served in two shifts. Leaving the mess hall after a hearty meal at the second table, Walt Randall saw that the teamsters, who had eaten at the first table, had hitched their draft horses to the wood-hauling wagons, had headed them up the newly completed road to the woodcutters' camp, and already were well past the junction of that road with the trail that led south over the ridge.

At the mine itself, Paddy Ryan and his crew of rock drillers, powder monkeys, and ore loaders, who also had eaten at the first table, were furiously at work in the tunnel. With only a few feet to go, they were eager to earn the half-day off promised them by Lord Smythe if they managed to punch through to daylight by noon. As a further bonus, he had offered them free beer and a card of prizefights topped by a match between Barney Breen and Paddy Ryan for a purse of one hundred dollars.

During breakfast, Allan, Barney, and Lord Smythe had engaged in a spirited discussion of the unloading problems that must be solved today. Heavy as those boilers were, swinging them off the boat's deck onto temporary cribbing placed on the sandbar could get deucedly sticky, Lord Smythe pointed out. But neither Allan nor Barney was concerned, each man expressing himself in his own peculiar *patois*.

"No sweat, Farley."

"A piece of cake, sir."

Walking down to the landing, where Barney was supervising the placing of timbers ashore while Allan oversaw the deckhands aboard as they rigged wire cables into slings with which to lift the boilers, Walt turned to Lord Smythe, who had paused beside him.

"Do you know what they're going to do?"

"More or less."

"Explain it to me, if you don't mind."

"Glad to, old chap. Those three poles they've planted between the boat and the cribbing will serve as an A-frame, giving them a great deal of leverage for a relatively small application of force. Once the boiler clears the deck, they'll swing it ashore—"

The sound of approaching horses made Lord Smythe break off and turn around. What he saw appeared to alarm him.

"I say, this may be trouble," he murmured to Walt. Raising his voice, he called out sharply to the boat, "Allan!"

"Yeah?"

"We have visitors."

Staring at the four men, who now were only a hundred feet away, Allan swore. "Vane and LeCroix! The dirty bastards! This time, I'll do more than dust their butts with birdshot!"

Leaping to the ladder, he climbed to the pilothouse, reached inside, and grabbed a double-barreled shotgun. As he swung it around, Frank Vane drew his pistol and fired. The bullet shattered the pilothouse window six inches above Allan's head. He froze.

"That's right," Vane grunted. "Mind your manners and don't point that scattergun at me. Put it back where you got it —or the next time I'll aim at your belly."

His face drained of color, Allan returned the shotgun to its place in the pilothouse. He glared at Vane.

"What in the hell are you up to?"

"We're going to borrow your boat, Allan, and go for a ride downriver."

"You're crazy!"

Vane smiled coldly. Motioning toward the mine tunnel, he said, "Zeke, Tom—go up to the tunnel and stand guard. The first man that comes outside, put a rifle slug two feet from his nose. Tell him to get back in the tunnel and keep his buddies in there with him. If anybody else comes out, shoot him."

"Gotcha, Frank."

Pulling repeating rifles out of saddle scabbards, Zeke Hewitt and Tom Crowell rode up the slope toward the entrance to the mine. As they neared it, Walt saw one of the workmen come out of the tunnel. Zeke Hewitt raised his rifle and fired. Shards of rock splintered out of the slope near the man's head.

Dropping to his knees, he rubbed his eyes with his hands, then stared at the two armed riders in bewilderment.

"What the hell—!"

"Git inside and stay there!" Hewitt yelled. "This is a holdup!"

Beside Frank Vane, Matt LeCroix had drawn his pistol and was watching the workmen on the sandbar while Vane covered the crew aboard the boat. Vane waved his pistol impatiently. "Get your men ashore and stop wastin' time."

After a moment's hesitation, Allan turned toward the stern of the boat and called down, "Scotty, Pete, Joe! Go ashore like the man says."

Casting sullen looks at Frank Vane, the chief engineer and the first and second mates came forward to the gangplank, walked ashore, and joined the group of workmen being held under guard on the sandbar.

"You, too," Vane snapped at Allan.

"Goddam you, Frank, you ain't got brains enough to pilot the *Angel!*" Allan exploded. "Loaded the way she is, it was all I could do to bring her upriver. You'll hole her bottom before you've gone five hundred yards!"

"It don't take brains to run a boat," Vane grunted contemptuously. "It just takes experience. I know the river almost as well as you do."

"Supposing you do make it to Lewiston. How are you going to explain stealing my boat to the people on the docks?"

"Why, I don't figure on stoppin' at Lewiston," Vane said. "So I won't have to explain nothin' to nobody. I figure to keep right on goin' downriver to The Dalles—"

"There isn't that much fuel on board."

"No, I didn't figure there would be. But there's places along the Snake and Columbia where a pilot can buy cordwood if he's got the cash. From what I hear, there's a carpetbag full of cash in the pilothouse."

"You bastard! So you know about the payroll!"

"You bet I do."

"You won't get away with it, Frank. Sooner or later, the law will run you down."

"With the head start we'll have, we'll take our chances on that," Vane grunted. "Now shut up and come ashore."

Reluctantly, Allan climbed down the ladder and crossed the gangplank to the sandbar. Herded by the two gunmen, Walt Randall, Allan, Lord Smythe, the boat crew, and the workmen walked up the slope to the entrance of the mine.

"Get inside," Vane said. "And tell your friends there'll be two rifles trained on the tunnel as long as the boat's in sight."

Despite the chagrin Walt felt for having been caught so completely off guard, he could not help but admire the audacity of the holdup. Its timing had been perfect. With the wood haulers gone and only the Chinese cook and his two helpers in the mess hall, every able-bodied man in camp now was bottled up in the mine tunnel. Steam pressure was up in the boat. If Vane were as skilled a pilot as he claimed to be, the *Angel* would reach Lewiston in three hours. But it would take at least three days for a man to hike there afoot over the steep, rugged, dangerous canyon trail that ran parallel to the river. By then, Vane and his cohorts would be far out of reach.

Standing just inside the tunnel entrance, Allan Randall, who was staring angrily down at the boat landing, gave a groan of dismay.

"The goddam fool! Don't he know better than to run a rapid stern first?"

"Is that what he's doing?" Walt asked.

"Yeah. He's had the mooring lines cast off but he's left the cable secured to the capstan. Looks like he intends to feed just enough power to the stern wheel to maintain steerageway, while he eases the *Angel* down through the rapid with the capstan."

"He probably feels that's the safest way."

"Safest way, hell! Loaded like she is, the *Angel*'s riding low by the stern. If she hits a rock, her paddle wheel and rudder will be the first things to go. Then she'll have neither steerageway nor power." Clenching his fists, he cried, "Lord, I wish I had a gun!"

"Faith, and it's no gun I can be givin' you," Paddy Ryan said politely at his elbow. "But I can give you something better."

"What?" Allan demanded, whirling around.

"Dynamite."

"By Jove, that's a capital idea, Paddy!" Lord Smythe exclaimed. "If we wrapped half a dozen sticks together, capped and fused them—"

"My powder monkeys are workin' on it now, sir. They'll have a nice little package ready in a couple of minutes."

"Great!" Allan said sarcastically. "But how do we deliver that nice little package? Is one of your powder monkeys willing to carry a capped dynamite bomb down the hill and heave it at the *Angel* while two men with rifles take potshots at him?"

"To tell the truth, sir, my thinkin' had not gone that far. Shall I ask for volunteers?"

"Don't bother wi' that, Paddy," Barney Breen muttered. "I'll deliver your package."

"No, you won't!" Allan said curtly. "I don't want you shot."

"Oh, I won't get shot, sir. I'll wait till the *Angel* gets around the bend, then I'll take the footpath up the side of the cliff on this side of the river—"

"That's a mighty steep climb, Barney. You'll have to go a hell of a long way before you get to a spot that overlooks the river. You'll never make it in time."

"They've left their 'orses at the landing, sir. I'll ride one of them."

"You're no horseman, Barney. You'd get thrown off the first jump."

"Then I'll go afoot, sir. But I'll run."

"Carrying a dynamite bomb you'll run up *that* path? No, Barney. I won't let you do it."

"May I ask a question?" Walt said.

"Sure."

"Would it be possible to place the dynamite bomb on a plank or raft that could be floated down the river and then detonated at the proper time?"

"Faith, and that'd be easy to do," Paddy said, nodding. "Of course, if the *Angel* is movin' downriver faster than the current is flowin', the bomb would never catch up with her."

"She's hardly moving at all," Allan said, as he gazed down the hill. "Vane is easing her into the rapid as slow as molasses in January."

"Then it could work," Lord Smythe said eagerly. "But we have two other problems to solve—balance and timing. If the plank or raft tips over—"

"It won't be a plank or raft," Paddy cut in. "We'll put the dynamite in an empty wooden nail keg and seal it."

"That's the ticket! How will you time the explosion?"

"We'll use contact detonators. They're waterproof and they won't go off till they hit something solid."

"Excellent! Put it together at once!" He turned to Allan, who was staring gloomily down the hill. "Is it safe to go outside now?"

"Yeah. She just cleared the bend."

As they hurried down the hill toward the empty landing, Walt looked inquiringly at Allan. "You don't think it will work, do you?"

"Oh, the dynamite will go off, all right," Allan answered with a shrug. "But who knows where? There's a thousand yards of rough water downriver. Floating free, that keg could be sucked into a whirlpool, tossed against a rock, or even go past the *Angel* without touching her. When the thing explodes, the odds are a hundred to one it won't be anywhere near where we want it to be."

"But you're going to give it a try, aren't you?"

"Yeah, I guess so. But, damn it, Walt, there's got to be a better way." Pausing at the river's edge, he suddenly seized Walt's arm. "Hey! Isn't that one of our Chinese friends from upriver?"

Washed ashore on the upper end of the sandbar was what

appeared to be the body of a slim, black-clad Chinaman. But even as the two men stared, the body stirred. As the head lifted, Walt realized that its owner was a girl, not a man.

"Ming!" he exclaimed. "What in the devil are you doing here?"

Leaping to her feet with a whimper of joy, she ran across the sandbar toward him.

"I find you, Mistah Walt, I find you!" she cried, and threw herself into his arms.

26

Surprised as Walt had been by the events of the past few minutes, there were even more shocking revelations to come. According to Ming's impassioned outburst, shortly after dawn Frank Vane and his three companions had murdered the eleven Chinamen who had been working on the sandbar half a mile upstream, stolen their gold, and thrown their bodies into the river. By a freak of fate, she had escaped and fled, seeking refuge here.

As he attempted to calm her, the workmen who had been bottled up in the mine tunnel were streaming down to the landing, angrily shaking their fists at the just-vanished boat and shouting imprecations at the thieves who had stolen their month's wages. Several of the more nimble men were running up the path that climbed the cliff on the west side of the river, seeking vantage points from which they could observe the progress of the *Hell's Angel* through the rapid.

Triumphantly bearing their improvised torpedo, Paddy Ryan and three of his powder monkeys carried the wooden nail keg down to the water's edge and gingerly set it on the sand. As the powder monkeys worked with the surehanded nonchalance of men accustomed to explosives, Paddy beamed with pride.

"You'll note, Lord Smythe, that we added a keel. That's to make sure the keg floats bottomside down. Note also, sir, that the boys are settin' detonators into its front, top, and sides. That's to make certain the charge will be triggered off no matter how the keg strikes the boat."

"Most ingenious, Paddy!" Lord Smythe exclaimed. "Her Majesty's Royal Navy could use you!"

"Beggin' your pardon, sir, but after servin' three years aboard a British man-of-war, I've had me fill of the Navy. Now into the U-bolt, which we've secured to the stern of the keg, the boys have tied ten feet of line, with a twelve-pound sash weight fastened to the other end. That weight should act like a sea anchor, sir, keepin' our little craft runnin' downstream bow first. Do you agree, Allan?"

"Sounds reasonable. How many sticks of dynamite did you put in the keg?"

"Twelve, sir. We saw no reason to underload this shot."

"If the charge goes off anywhere near the boat, it'll do the job," Allan said. "We'll just have to hope for a lucky hit."

Watching Paddy Ryan and the three powder monkeys ease the keg into the water, Ming asked curiously, "What are they doing?"

"They've made up a dynamite bomb," Walt said. "They're going to float it down the river toward the boat."

"What if it misses boat?"

"Then nothing happens."

"And bandits get away?"

"Afraid so."

Gazing across the river at the taut, quivering steel cable to which the slow-moving boat was attached as it was cautiously eased into the rapid, Ming asked innocently, "Mistah Walt, why not slide bomb down cable?"

"Sure, that'd work fine," Allan said sardonically. "If we could get to the cable. But we don't have a boat—"

"I can get to cable."

Allan stared at her dubiously. "How?"

"Swim to it."

"She is a good swimmer," Walt said. "She was born and raised on water."

"She can't swim here, Walt. Nobody can swim the Snake in this part of the canyon."

"But I swim here," Ming said. "I swim here many times."

"When?"

"Every day for three months I work on bottom as diver. Twice each week I swim across and back after dark. Just now, I swim half mile down river. Look at me. Do I breathe hard?"

"By Jove, she's not breathing hard!" Lord Smythe exclaimed, staring at her in amazement. "What a remarkable performance!"

"She's a remarkable young lady," Walt said quietly.

"I'll vouch for that," Allan murmured. He looked at her intently for a moment, then said, "Do you really want to do this, Ming?"

"For Mistah Walt, I do anything," she said firmly. "Like I tell you after he get shot, I love him."

"What about you, Walt?" Allan asked. "Are you willing to let her risk it?"

"If she thinks she can do it, yes. And she says she can."

"All right. We'll give it a try."

At the head of the sandbar on which the Golden Girl camp was located, the Snake was three hundred feet wide, its blue-green surface broken by slicks, boils, and whirlpools that were moving with deceptive swiftness toward the rapid downstream. There, towering basaltic cliffs on either side compressed the tremendous volume of the river into a space barely sixty feet wide. Literally turning on edge as it entered the narrow canyon, the Snake went mad for the next quarter mile, its foaming white water too light to support a swimmer's body, its force too powerful to be resisted. If sucked into the chute at the head of the rapid, no human body could possibly survive the passage through the turbulent stretch of river to the quieter reaches below.

A hasty search of the camp supply tent produced only five hundred feet of half-inch rope. Because of the current's force, Allan felt that this was the lightest rope that would hold her weight without breaking.

As he passed the rope end around her body, he asked, "Where do you want the loop tied—under your armpits or around your waist?"

"Around waist."

"Okay—raise your arms."

Pushing his hands away as he started to put the rope around the outside of her soaked black cotton jacket, she lifted the lower skirt of the jacket so that a generous expanse of bare skin was revealed.

"Under jacket, not over. Not loose, not tight."

"That about right?"

"Yes. That fine."

"This is a bowline, Ming, a kind of knot that won't tighten up, no matter how much strain we put on the rope. It'll be easy to untie, once you get across. Just pull here—"

"I know. Chinese boat people tie same knot."

"We'll pay out line from the sandbar as you swim across. If you make it to the rock where the cable is secured, untie the line from around your waist and fasten it to the cable. When it's in place, clap your hands together twice—like this—and we'll turn the torpedo loose. Do you understand?"

"Yes."

"Between here and the head of the rapid, the current picks up speed awfully fast. If we see you've got no chance to reach the rock, we'll start hauling you back—"

"I will make it. Leave me alone and I will make it."

"We're not going to leave you alone if you get in trouble, Ming," Walt said sharply.

"Once the rapid takes hold of you, it won't let you go," Allan said. "The rope isn't strong enough to hold you in that kind of water. When you feel us pull, don't fight. Turn back toward this bank, keep your head above water, and we'll haul you in. Are you ready?"

"No. Not quite."

"What's wrong?" Walt asked with sudden concern.

"Wet clothes no good," Ming said, a twinkle coming into her eyes. "Don't look, please."

Unbuttoning her jacket, she slipped it off; unfastening her pantaloons, she stepped out of them. Stark naked now, she tossed Walt her discarded clothes, turned and ran toward the river, laughing gaily. "Swim in skin like fish! Now you can look!"

As an old China hand, Lord Smythe was not nearly as astonished at her sudden disrobing as were Walt, Allan, and the other men standing on the sandbar. But it was he who transformed their spontaneous shouts of approval, as she dove into the river and started swimming strongly toward the Idaho shore, into a more formal tribute to her courage. Turning toward the workmen, he raised his hands like a band conductor and shouted: "Let's hear it for the young lady, lads! Three cheers and a tiger!"

By the time the *Hip-Hip-Hoorays!* had stopped echoing and re-echoing off the steep walls of the canyon, Ming Sen was halfway across the river. Swimming with no wasted effort, she was still well upstream from the rock where the deadman was set. But the length of rope trailing in the water behind her was becoming a burden to her now as it bellied downstream. Watching Allan pay it out, Lord Smythe moved to his side and gave him a flip-wristed hand gesture sure to be understood by any fly-fisherman.

"Mend your line upstream, old chap. It'll save her a bit of drag."

"Should have thought of that myself," Allan muttered. "Tend the coil for me."

Getting to his feet with half a dozen loops of rope in his hands, he moved upstream to the base of the ridge. As Ming needed slack, he tossed as big a half circle of rope as he could handle upriver. Lord Smythe nodded approval. When casting across a fast-flowing river, upstream line mending let a fly dropped in a likely looking spot linger there for a few extra seconds before the line bellying downstream pulled it away—precious seconds that often produced a strike by a big trout or salmon. In the present endeavor, the same trick might save their swimmer just enough strength to succeed rather than fail.

"Faith, and I do believe she's goin' to make it!" Paddy Ryan murmured. "Stand by to launch the torpedo!"

"She's moving downstream awfully fast," Walt Randall said anxiously. "Has she lost too much headway, Allan?"

"It's gonna be close. Yell when you run out of line, Farley."

"That I will."

Taking advantage of a swirling eddy whose upstream arc thrust toward the Idaho shore, Ming had progressed to within ten feet of the far bank when a strong downstream current caught her. For several agonizing seconds she made no forward movement at all, though she obviously was swimming with all her strength. With the increasingly powerful current thrusting her downstream, she was still a good arm's reach away from the rock when the water washed her past it.

"She's not gonna make it!" Allan yelled. "Haul her in, Farley! Haul her in!"

Leaping to his feet, Lord Smythe took a quick wrap of the rope around his buttocks and leaned back against it as a human deadman. Walt hurried to him, seized the rope in front of him, and started to pull. Feeling the rope grow taut, Ming turned in the water, waved a hand at him in a sharp negative gesture, then faced again toward the Idaho shore.

Though there was no possibility of her reaching the rock now, Walt shouted at Farley, "She wants slack! Give her slack!"

Lord Smythe let ten feet of rope slip through his hands and burn around his buttocks, then clamped down again with his hands, dug his heels into the sand, and leaned back. Allan came running toward them, livid with anger.

"Goddam it, you're gonna drown her! Haul in, I say! *Haul her in!*"

Indeed, she had disappeared from sight, Walt saw with sudden panic. Had she suffered a cramp? Had she collapsed of exhaustion? No, there she was, twenty feet downstream from the rock. But she no longer was being pushed along by the current. She was holding her own. By God, she was swimming *upstream*, toward the rock. Which was odd, for her arms were barely moving and her hands were out of sight underwater. In fact, it looked like she was crawling. . . .

"She's caught hold of the cable!" Allan screamed hoarsely. "She's moving up it hand over hand! Give her some slack, goddam it! Give her some slack!"

"Make up your mind!" Walt shouted, but he was laughing with sheer joy. "'Atta girl, Ming. 'Atta girl!"

She had reached the rock now. Pulling herself out of the water, she undid the loop from around her waist, made a quick tie around the cable, held it up so that Allan could see it, then clapped her hands together twice.

This time, the cheers of the workmen on the sandbar were informal, but their volume made up for the lack of a leader. Securing the near end of the line to the U-bolt fastened to the stern of the nail keg, Paddy Ryan jumped to his feet, clicked his heels together, and brought his right hand smartly up to his forehead in what any officer in Her Majesty's Royal Navy surely would have called a quite proper salute.

"Torpedo ready to launch, sir!"

"Let 'er go!" Allan cried.

Eased into the water by its proud creators, the remodeled nail keg started its journey downriver. As a final touch, one of the powder monkeys had tied a red bandana handkerchief to a wooden rod and fastened it to the top side of the keg as a flagstaff. Watching the little craft move along, Lord Smythe held up an imaginary champagne glass and called downriver, "*Bon voyage*, gentlemen—wherever you may land!"

"Up yours!" Paddy cried inelegantly.

"Fire in the 'ole!" Barney Breen yelled. "You'll get a bang out of this!"

"See you around, boys!" Allan shouted. "And around . . . and around . . . and around . . . !"

As the nail keg and its fluttering red flag disappeared beyond the bend downstream, Allan turned and started running toward the path up the steep cliff on the west side of the river. "C'mon, fellas! If we hustle, we can see her when she blows!"

Shouting and laughing like boys bound for a Fourth of July fireworks display, the workmen scrambled up the path as fast as they could go, led by Allan, Paddy, Barney, and Lord Smythe. Because of the steepness of the climb, Lord Smythe had to stop part way up the slope, letting the others move past him while he caught his breath. Looking back and down, he saw that Walt had stayed behind. Alone on the sandbar, he was peering anxiously out across the river.

Following the direction of his gaze, Lord Smythe was astonished to see that Ming had not remained on the Idaho side of the Snake for even a few minutes' recuperation from her exertions. Instead, she had plunged back into the river and was swimming toward the Oregon shore. With no safety line around her waist and no help available to her if she got in trouble, it was understandable that Walt should be concerned.

He need not have been. Even as Lord Smythe watched, she reached the shallows adjacent to the sandbar, came up out of the water, and ran laughing into Walt's arms. As he enfolded her slim, glistening body, it did not appear to trouble him in the least that she was stark naked and dripping wet. . . .

27

Although Ming was not at all abashed by her nakedness, Walt insisted that she put on her clothes.

"I've got something to tell you," he said firmly. "But I can't concentrate on what I'm saying when you're undressed. You distract me."

"I've got something to tell you, too," Ming said, giggling happily as she stepped into her pantaloons and put on her jacket. "There is much gold hidden—"

"I've missed you terribly, Ming. You never should have gone away. I won't let you do it again—"

"It is in a cave—"

"I'm going to marry you, Ming. Legal or not, we're going to live together as man and wife—"

"I am the only one who knows where the cave is—"

"Ming, I love you. Are you listening to me?"

"And I love you," she murmured, kissing him again.

Turning away, she pointed at a spot halfway up the slope on the Idaho side of the river. "See that big black rock? The one that hangs over the slide?"

"Sure," Walt said. "In fact, that's what it's called—Hangover Rock."

"You know about it, then?"

"Only what Allan has told me. It was named after a prospector, he says, who went on a spree one night and felt like hell the next morning. What about it?"

"Under it is a cave. That is where I hid the gold."

"What gold?"

"The gold I dug underwater. Ah Fat said we must keep it

secret from the others. He was going to kill me, I think, and take it all for himself."

"How much gold?"

"I hid many sacks in the cave. I think fifty thousand dollars' worth."

"Oh, come on, Ming! That's impossible!"

"Is possible. Listen to me . . ."

Walt listened incredulously as she told him of her find. When she had finished, he exclaimed, "Ming, you're a jewel! Why, if you managed to recover that much gold working underwater alone, there must be a fortune in that pool. Lord Smythe will know how to get it out. With a dredge, maybe—"

Muffled by distance and the steep terrain, there came the sound of an explosion. Wheeling around, Walt stared downriver.

"The torpedo! I wonder if it got them . . . ?"

Badly winded by his run along the winding, narrow path, Lord Smythe caught up with the others several hundred yards downriver. Here, a rocky promontory jutting out from the Oregon side of the canyon gave an unobstructed view of the churning white waters of the rapid below. Staring down at the *Hell's Angel*, which had slowed to a near standstill as its pilot debated which of two channels to take around a cluster of dark brown rocks, Allan Randall was waving his arms and cursing Vane's indecision.

"Keep to the left, damn it! Can't you see that's where the deep water is?"

"Got the torpedo spotted, Paddy?" Barney Breen asked.

"Aye, I just now found her!" Paddy Ryan muttered as he peered through a pair of binoculars he had scrounged from somewhere. "She's on course an' sailin' steady!"

"'Ow far does she 'ave left to go?"

"A hundred yards—an' closin' fast. What a darlin' craft she is! You done yourselves proud, boys!"

"Now you've got it!" Allan shouted down at the boat, ignoring the fact that he could not be heard over the noise of the engine and the thunder of the rapids. "Cut off your power before you go over that shelf! Let her drift, you idiot! Ease her down! Ease her—!"

"Fifty yards!" Paddy cried. "Forty! Thirty—!"

Turning to stare at the rock-drilling foreman, Allan Randall suddenly went pale. As if realizing for the first time that in order to stop the men who had stolen his boat, he must destroy the boat itself, he grabbed Paddy by the arm and shook him fiercely.

"How many sticks of dynamite did you say you put in that keg?"

"Twelve, sir."

"Good God! You'll make kindling wood of the *Angel!*"

"You wanted them blasted, didn't you?"

"The men, sure. But I didn't want to blow up my boat! I put my life's blood into—!"

Below them, the *Hell's Angel* suddenly disintegrated. A fraction of a second later, a tremendous blast shattered the air. Instinctively dropping to the ground, Lord Smythe and the workmen covered their ears and eyes and laid flat, protecting their heads from the shower of debris that normally could be expected to rain down following such a powerful shot.

Since the river lay several hundred feet below the promontory and the canyon walls on either side were almost vertical, little fallout reached this spot. But a tremendous concussion rumbled up the canyon, echoing and re-echoing, building in volume as it expanded. When the sound had died away, Lord Smythe got to his feet and moved to the outer edge of the bluff. His shoulders sagging, his eyes filled with tears, Allan Randall stood staring despondently down into the canyon, where a haze of smoke and rock dust obscured the shattered remains of the *Hell's Angel*.

"I didn't mean to kill her, Farley!" he said brokenly. "I didn't mean to kill her . . . !"

"I know, lad," Lord Smythe said gently, patting him on

the shoulder. "Don't grieve for her. We'll build another boat. . . ."

Standing on the sandbar with Ming Sen, Walt Randall heard the sound of the explosion a quarter of a mile downriver as it rolled toward them. Following the windings of the canyon, the sound waves passed over them, dwindled, then died away as they moved around the bend upstream. For a moment, there was a silence. Then there came a rumble, like the beginnings of an earthquake. Underfoot, the sandbar quivered perceptibly.

High up on the canyon wall on the Idaho side of the river, a piece of basaltic rimrock collapsed and dropped toward the water three thousand feet below.

From this distance, it looked to be inconsequential in size. In reality, it weighed thousands of tons. Gathering speed as it fell, it struck the steep slope and bounced half a dozen times before it came to rest in the river. Each time it hit, a rock slide of ever-increasing proportion began. Dust filled the air; the noise became deafening; the whole massive wall of the canyon appeared to be breaking up and falling. Beside him, Ming was pulling at his arm and screaming frantically.

"The rock above the cave, Mistah Walt! It's moving!"

Indeed, Hangover Rock *was* moving, Walt noted with the calm sense of detachment that comes to a person when he is forced to view a cataclysm of nature that he cannot control. In fact, the entire Idaho side of the canyon was tumbling down into the river—obliterating the cave in which Ming had hidden the gold, filling up the pool in which she had made her find, and changing the physical appearance of this part of Snake River into unrecognizable chaos, just as, in eons past, the physical appearance of Hell's Canyon had been changed many times before.

At long last, the rocks stopped sliding, the rumbling noises ceased, and only the quiet, murmuring sounds of the river could be heard. Wide-eyed with wonder and fear, Ming clung to him.

J 19

"Is it an omen, Mistah Walt?" she whispered. "Are the gods angry because we love each other? Are they telling us we are wrong to marry?"

"No, of course not," he answered softly, as he smiled and stroked her still-damp hair. "They're just having their little joke. Can't you hear them laughing?"